ROTATION
PLAN

Dead Man Riding

Two years before, Logan Priest had left the woman he loved in the hope of sheltering her from the dangers of his profession . . . but he made a terrible mistake. When a vicious outlaw whom he brought to justice escapes prison, he seeks revenge on the very woman that Priest once sought to protect.

Logan has no desire to return to the manhunting trail until he receives the outlaw's grisly calling-card.

Can he gather his wits in time to meet the challenge or will he become the killer's next victim?

Dead Man Riding

Lance Howard

A Black Horse Western

ROBERT HALE · LONDON

© Howard Hopkins 2010
First published in Great Britain 2010

ISBN 978-0-7090-8944-5

Robert Hale Limited
Clerkenwell House
Clerkenwell Green
London EC1R 0HT

www.halebooks.com

Typeset by
Derek Doyle & Associates, Shaw Heath
Printed and bound in Great Britain by
CPI Antony Rowe, Chippenham and Eastbourne

For Tannenbaum

Please visit Lance Howard on the web at
www.howardhopkins.com

CHAPTER ONE

Even after two years, Serena Hedison still missed that man. She reckoned a week didn't pass when he wasn't riding through her dreams.

No, that wasn't quite right now, was it? He wasn't riding through her dreams; he was riding away from her in them. Away from her and away from the life he'd promised they would one day share *together* on this small ranch.

She plunged the hoe into the moist spring ground, the thrust coming with more anger than she imagined she should still be holding onto after such a long spell. He was gone, and that's all there was to it. Longing and anger would not bring him back, would never change his mind.

For Logan Priest was nothing if not a stubborn man.

A trickle of sweat meandered from her forehead and traced a path down her face, which was flushed with crimson. Dressed in a plain skirt and a blouse stained with soil and sweat, she'd been tending this small garden since dawn and the sun, now blazing high above the hilly horizon, beat down on her like Satan's own fire. Its glaring heat had chased away the chill of the night and glazed the grassland and stands of cottonwood with shimmery emerald, but had not vanquished the chill of loneliness and regret embedded in her soul.

The scent of lilacs from a cluster of bushes planted at each corner of the clapboard-sided ranch house perfumed the air and teased her nostrils. Somewhere, birds were twittering up a storm. A gentle breeze stirred the corkscrew strands of auburn hair that twirled from beneath her blue kerchief to either side of her face. Her brown eyes, lined prematurely – missing someone you loved powerfully will do that to you, she reckoned – narrowed to a squint against the sun's glare as her gaze swept out over the parcel of land she used to hope would be theirs.

It all felt so ... serene. A perfect spring day. Except for one thing.

Darkness.

Was that the right word? Yes, she was certain it was, indeed, though she had no earthly notion why it should be. Darkness, as if something bleak and foreboding permeated the air, invisible and haunting, stalking and inevitable. Something from the past?

Perhaps. But whatever caused that word to invade her mind it was more than something external, for it came also from within, sweeping over her in brief yet intense waves.

Darkness. On a warm, sunlit spring day. On a perfect day . . . an imperfection.

She shook her head and drew a deep breath, trying to force her mind away from the uncomfortable sensation crawling through her innards.

Hands gripping the handle tight enough to ache, she plunged the hoe into the earth again, still mocked by a joker of anger. Anger came, anger went. It had done so for two years. She reckoned by now she should be used to it, should be over it.

But how did one get over something lost when that something meant everything?

She'd asked herself that question a thousand times, never once settling upon a suitable answer.

He's gone! she chastised herself, not sure whether she was more angry at him and his excuses, or herself for clutching to a dream that was never to be.

Gone. Forever. He was never coming back.

'It's for your own good,' he had told her the day she watched him ride off, his head never turning to look back, his heart never reconsidering. As if all they had shared, every raw emotion, every tender touch, every whispered secret, meant nothing at all.

9

Perhaps they hadn't. To him.

But to her? To her they had meant the world.

Silly excuses. A man in his line of work . . . well, she reckoned manhunting did indeed come with its share of hazards, dangers, enemies. But how likely was it one of those enemies from his past would ever bother them? How would someone bent on revenge even find them in an isolated little Colorado town such as this? She supposed there were ways, but hadn't the perpetual threat of danger, of death, been hers to accept or decline?

She told him as much, but he had claimed otherwise. He had told her he would protect her, even if she refused that protection. By riding out of her life forever.

'You sonofabitch,' she whispered, anger rushing through her blood in a dark wave. 'Why didn't you let me make that choice?'

Tears flooded her eyes and she had all she could do to hold them back. She'd told herself she would no longer cry, no longer miss him, no longer mourn what might have been.

She had told herself many such lies over the past couple of years.

'Logan Priest, I hate you!' she shouted and flung the hoe to the ground. 'Damn you!' Her hands balled into fists capped with white knuckles. Emotion shuddered through her entire body.

This was getting her nowhere. Why couldn't she

simply move on with her life? Why couldn't she just forget him?

Because something had been left unfinished, the thought came back to her. Something. . . .

Was coming.

Darkness.

Again, a chill swept over her, black and acute, shivering through every cell. What was wrong with her? She'd experienced strange feelings in the past, premonitions almost, of impending danger, but never anything this strong, this palpable. Mostly, she'd ignored them, chalking them up to fatigue or possibly even a sign that the loneliness was making her crazy or paranoid. A woman on her own was perfect prey for Indian and outlaw alike. . . .

A sound penetrated her reverie.

A hoof beat? Yes, a hoof beat. Coming from. . . .

Behind her.

She whirled and he was there, as if he had simply materialized out of thin air, his shape black as a raven, backlit by morning sunlight, a battered hat pulled low on his forehead. A wild beard covered his lower face but wilder still were his dark eyes, which somehow seemed to blaze ebony from the shadows slicing across his face.

For a moment, he didn't move, merely stared down at her, as if studying her like a snake studies a mouse. One hand clutched the reins; the other was occupied with some sort of timepiece he kept

11

turning over in his palm.

'Who . . . who are you?' Her voice came more unsteady than she would have liked. She reckoned she didn't even need an answer. She knew who he was, if not in name. He was Evil made flesh. He was the past come back, the emissary of the darkness she had felt pervading the air, her soul.

He was the very thing from which Logan had sought to protect her.

And now he was here, this being of evil, some outlaw from Logan's past. Somehow he had made a connection between them and found her. And that meant nothing good.

She uttered a gasp, every muscle in her body going rigid. She couldn't help it. The very sight of this man chilled her to the bone. Call it second sight or plain panic, this man was here to kill her.

'I done waited a long time to find you . . .' the man spoke, his voice like she imagined the Devil's would be. 'A very long time.'

'What do you want?' She struggled to steady her voice, having little success.

He tucked the timepiece into a vest pocket beneath his duster, then licked his lips. 'Reckon that's plain, missy.'

'No, sir, indeed it is not.' She forced herself to hold her ground, her chin coming forward, her bosom lifting. 'This is my land and I want you off of it. Please leave now.'

A low laugh trickled from his thin lips and he swung down from the saddle. 'Then let me make it such,' he said as his black duster swept back to reveal a Bowie knife sheathed at one hip, a Smith & Wesson holstered at the other. 'You see, me an' your man . . . we got ourselves a reckoning. You're his invite—'

Something in her belly plunged. This man was here to use her against Logan in some horrible way she felt certain meant her death.

Panic overtaking her, she lunged, grabbed the hoe, came up with it. Whirling, she swung the tool. The handle caught the man a sideways blow on the shoulder as he tried to step out of the way. He staggered to his left and she swung the hoe again, slamming it into his side.

He groaned, hesitated, but didn't go down. She dropped the implement and whirled, bolted for the house.

Her heart pounded in her throat and her breath beat out in searing gasps. A fluttery sensation overtook her legs, making her stumble and nearly plunge headlong to the ground. She wasn't certain how she managed to stay upright.

Behind her, the man yelled something, the words lost in the thundering of her pulse in her ears.

Only a few more yards to her door. Only a few more feet to sanctuary, to a rifle that rested on pegs above her fireplace mantle.

He had stopped shouting and was charging after

13

her now. His heavy bootfalls penetrated the thrumming in her ears as if they were gunshots.

She reached the porch, clambered up the three steps. *Please let me reach the Winchester,* she thought, her heart banging harder, her head swimming.

A thought flashed through her mind, one that confirmed that Logan had been wrong to try to protect her by leaving. It hadn't mattered, had it? The evil had still found her and still aimed to kill her. If he had stayed, perhaps he could have protected her, perhaps he *could* have stopped this devil of a man. Logan had made a mistake, and now both of them were going to pay dearly for it, unless she reached that rifle.

She crossed the porch in a bound, plunged into the ranch house and swung the door shut, even as the man clomped up the steps. An inarticulate noise of fright escaped her lips as she threw the bolt.

She dashed across the small parlor, a flood of relief washing over her. She grabbed the Winchester, yanked it from its pegs and whisked it around just as a crash reverberated from the door. A boot slamming against wood, she guessed.

The door shuddered, but held, and she lifted the rifle, aiming straight at the entrance. Its heaviness felt comforting in her small hands, a savior of steel and gunpowder.

Another crash sounded and the lock splintered, but still the door held.

14

'I love you, Logan,' she murmured, lips quivering. 'I always have and I always will.'

A third crash thundered and the bolt tore completely from the wall. The door bounded inward slamming against the opposite wall, rebounding. He stopped it with the heel of his hand, sent it swinging inward again. Then he poised there, a demon backlit by sunlight.

'It'll be easier if'n you don't put up a fight.' A grin swelled on his lips, and he stepped into the parlor.

'Don't!' she snapped, jerking the rifle towards him.

He hesitated, as if contemplating whether he could cross the room and reach her before she pulled the trigger.

'Not fast enough,' she answered, divining his thoughts.

'No, I suppose not,' he said.

Why was he so damnably confident, so utterly unafraid of her? His demeanor, his stance, nothing indicated that of a man with a rifle held on him. Was this man totally without fear? Was he so wholly evil bullets would have no effect on him?

It dawned on her, then, as she caught the flick of his gaze beneath his hat, the gaze that went to the fireplace mantle, then back to her in a heartbeat.

She knew. Oh, yes, she knew now why he was unafraid. He was taking a calculated risk, a guess, because from the corner of her eye she could see what he'd glanced at, a box of rifle shells resting on the mantle.

'Oh, no,' she muttered, working the lever and pulling the trigger out of reflex.

An empty clack foretold her fate.

His laugh filled the parlor, an expression of almost sentient, living evil. He came forward, his hand sweeping to the Bowie knife at his wasit and freeing it from its sheath.

She hurled the rifle at him with all her might, but he sidestepped it so easily she had the fleeting impression it passed right through him.

She glanced about, searching for something with which to defend herself, then grabbed the fireplace poker. But before she could swing it he snatched it from her hand and hurled it aside.

'No, please,' she muttered, her voice like a drowning kitten's.

'Ain't personal, you understand that, don't you?' he said. 'I jest need to know what makes him tick. An' I need to break him.' He jerked up the knife and brought it down in a slashing arc. 'Plus I just plain enjoy killin'.'

CHAPTER TWO

You're a mule-headed fool, Logan Priest assured himself for not the first time in the last two years. Not the hundredth time, either. Perhaps not even the thousandth. He'd lost count ages ago and could no longer recollect how many times he'd chastised himself for making the biggest mistake of his life. He rightly supposed the count didn't matter. Branding yourself a fool came with no numerical limitations nor any constraints on guilt. A fool was a fool and always would be, and the man staring back at him from the reflection in his whiskey glass was a fool of the first measure.

For a dragging moment, the bar room vanished about him and he saw only that haggard reflection, the likeness of a face young but battered by the elements, nature and emotion. Deep lines webbed from the corners of his pale-gray eyes and dark half-circles nested beneath them. His face appeared slightly sallow, the result of too little time spent in

17

the sunlight and too much occupying a seat in any of a hundred bar rooms across Colorado Territory. Most days he spent his time feeling sorry for himself and most nights he conversed with Dr Whiskey, all the while pissing away the money he'd banked from his manhunting days, days now two years buried in the shallow grave of his memory.

He wished to hell he could bury other things the way he had his former career, but some memories . . . some memories could never be laid to rest and Selena Hedison's was one of them. The image of his own face in the alcohol blurred and another took its place: hers. Her soft auburn hair flowed about her exquisite face, and her brown eyes filled with hurt and heartbreak stared back at him the way a condemned man stares at his executioner. Sorrow, loneliness, guilt boiled up inside him and made him shudder.

Whiskey couldn't numb what he had lost, couldn't blunt the pain. He should have known better. He'd spent two years trying to no avail, though he'd done a damned fine job of throwing away his pride and dignity.

But none of that mattered to a man waiting to die.

No, that was not entirely correct, was it? For all intents, he had died two years ago. Physically, he remained, but his reason for being had long passed. It had deserted him the day he rode away from Serena and didn't look back, though everything within his being had cried out for him to turn around. Had he but glanced back at her saddened face he never would have been able to leave, when, to his way of thinking, it was written in stone that he must.

For her own good. That's what he had told her. To protect her from outlaws bent on revenge, men from his past who had no loftier notion other than to get even with the manhunter who had put them away.

He could recollect clearly one man in particular, one he feared would one day find a way out of jail and likely be focused on nothing except revenge upon the man who'd brought him to justice. That man was like a rabid animal, and amongst Logan's many regrets was a burning conviction that told him that man should never have been brought to trial and left to rotting in a cell. That man should have been put down. But in those days Logan Priest had clung to some shred of his morality, some spark of his humanity that no longer seemed to plague him. That man would come for him one of these days. And the way his skills had eroded, he doubted he'd even see the bullet coming.

Had he made the right choice, leaving her? Was it truly the biggest mistake of his life or the loftiest sacrifice? She was happy by now, he reckoned, free to live without constant worry or fear of the past coming back on them. She'd probably long ago forgotten him.

The way you forgot her?

You gave her no choice, you damned fool, he chastised himself. She hadn't wanted him to leave. In fact, she had begged him to stay. But Logan Priest was nothing if not a stubborn man. She'd informed him of that countless times and the thought of it brought a flicker of a smile to his lips, a rare emotion these days.

He wondered how she was doing, if she had married, settled into that small ranch she owned. Numerous times he'd considered riding out there, to check on her, but always talked himself out of it. He knew better, because to see her again might shatter the resolve he'd so painstakingly fostered – faked? – all this time. And to see her with another man ... well, that would just feel like a blade twisting in his heart.

'You can't have it both ways,' he told himself in a whisper, as the image of her face in the whiskey dissolved and he came from his thoughts. 'You can't have it any way. . . .'

He wasn't entirely sure what had nudged him from the mire of his thoughts, as through bleary eyes he saw the bar room materialize around him. He'd shut it all out, the noise, glasses and silver pieces clinking, raucous shouts and continual bantering; cowboys playing poker, chuck-a-luck and faro; bargirls leaning over winners' shoulders, their bosoms mounding from their sateen tops and their soft chuckles punctuating honey-coated proposals. He managed to focus, realizing some of it was the Durham haze hanging in the air and not his vision that was cloudy.

'I asked if you wanted some company, sugar?' a soft voice came from beside him, and suddenly he realized what had spoiled his dark reverie.

A bargirl stood beside him, her hand resting on his shoulder. Dressed in a blue sateen bodice and frilly skirt, her cheeks daubed with too much coral and her eyes darkened with too much kohl, she cast him a lascivious eye and he wondered what the hell possessed her. He was used to being left alone and damned well preferred it that way. A faint inner voice reprimanded him for letting the woman sneak up on him; two years ago that never would have happened.

'Go away,' he said, his voice hard-edged, brooking no argument.

Her face took on a hurt look that carried all the sincerity of a wooden nickel.

'Why, sugar, I'm just lookin' to cheer you up.' She gave him a sly smile, one that promised soft whispers and sinful pleasures most men would have had no desire or ability to resist. She was probably the prettiest whore in the saloon, with her curls of red hair, though her blue eyes were clouded with a laudanum mist. But he hadn't touched another

21

woman in two years. None could compare to Serena, so why bother?

'Reckon I told you to get the hell away from me,' he said, irritation prickling his hide. 'Won't tell you again.'

The look that flashed across her warpainted features this time was genuine and altogether annoyed. A sliver of viciousness glinted in her eyes. He reckoned she wasn't the type to back off, either, because she showed no fear of him, and most folks did when he got into one of his moods, which was pretty regularlike.

'You got a hell of a nerve, cowboy, you know that?' She backed up a step, removing her hand from his shoulder as if she'd grabbed a hot skillet. She balled her fists and jammed them into her full hips. 'You come in here everyday for the past week and fall into your sorry little world and mope about all pitiful-like and you got the gall to turn me down? You're on some mighty high horse for a no-good drunk, ain't you?'

It surprised him he had pissed her off so thoroughly; this gal had some kind of chip on her shoulder that apparently didn't allow her to accept rejection.

'I ain't a drunk,' he felt compelled to say in a defensive tone, though he couldn't reckon for what reason her accusation had prickled him.

She cast him a spiteful smile, looked him up and

22

down, then glanced at the half-empty whiskey bottle. Gaze sharp and condemning, she shook her head.

'Oh, no? Can't tell by me, gent. I see you put down half a bottle or more every night for a week and walk on outa here like you'd been drinkin' sarsaparilla. Tolerance like that paints you as either a drunk or an idiot.'

He was inclined to go with the latter, though it wasn't much of an upgrade. His pale-gray eyes narrowed on her, resentment washing into them.

'I reckon my libation limit ain't none of your concern. I also reckon you been watching me pass the barkeep double eagles for the past week to buy me a bottle and some privacy and figgered you'd take advantage of my generosity.'

A startled look flickered across her features, proving he had pegged her right, and she didn't care for it one lick. An instant later, she slapped him, confirming his notion. Slapped him hard. His head rocked and his cheek stung and he was half-inclined to spring out of his chair and slap her back, but refrained.

'Like I said, get the hell away from me.' His voice had lowered and this time she took a backwards step, seeing something in his eyes that made her wary, and rightly so. He had his limits and with each passing day the leash on them got shorter.

She pranced away, glancing back once with a haughty flip of her hair, before finding another mark.

He sighed, grabbing the bottle and pouring more whiskey into his glass. He'd been in this damned town for only a week and already he'd worn out his welcome. Sonofabitch.

After setting the bottle down and lifting his glass to his lips, he took a gulp, wondering for an instant if she weren't right, that maybe he had become nothing more than a pathetic drunk. The whiskey barely touched him now. It took more and more to reach a level where the guilt and loneliness lost their edge.

Hell, it didn't matter what he was now, anyway. For Logan Priest was a man with no future and he had long ago accepted that fact.

A sound disturbed his thoughts again, and anger rushed through his veins as he looked up to see a young man standing before his table. Dammit, he sure as hell had become the star attraction in town tonight, hadn't he?

'What the hell you want?' he jabbed at the young man with tousled blond hair and a skinny frame. This lad was afraid of him, he could see it in his eyes, and that struck him as funny for no particular reason other than meanness.

'I was sent here with a package for you. Came on the stage an hour ago.'

For the first time Logan noticed the boy was holding a wooden box roughly 18 by 18 inches. The thing was made out of mahogany if he figured right and a small gold plaque was secured to its top. The boy placed the box on the table.

'How the hell anyone know I was here? Or who I am?' A vague suspicion, some kind of sixth sense left over from his manhunter days surfaced. Something felt . . . *wrong*. Perhaps if he hadn't been so lubricated he might have paid it more heed.

The boy's lips worked but no sound came out.

'Goddammit, out with it!' Logan snapped. 'I ain't a patient man.'

'Everybody knows where you are since you came to town. Some folks recognized you, back from, well, you know, when, when you was in them novels.'

Logan sighed. That's right. He had carried a fierce reputation once, had been a dime novel hero briefly, much to his consternation. Those stories had damn near got his head shot off by greenhorns looking to make a name and gunmen looking to further their reputation. That had all played into his decision to leave Serena, hadn't it?

He fished in a pocket, then flipped a silver dollar onto the table. The boy snatched it up, spun and darted for the batwings. Logan almost laughed, but something about the box stifled that emotion.

This was no laughing matter, was it?

Some dark notion penetrated his brain, informing him he was still too damnably alive and still all too capable of being hurt. He stared at the box, the dark feeling swelling.

Who would know he was here, given his itinerant ways?

Someone following, observing . . . seeking something.

What?

Revenge.

'No,' he muttered, gaze focusing on the gold plaque, which held words that sent a sobering chill through him.

Resting in Pieces, the legend said, and imprinted below it the initials: *DM.*

For the first time in two years Logan Priest began to shake. Only this time the tremors came not from his heart breaking but from a terrible dark fear that told him the past had come a-callin' and though he had considered himself a man long dead, he was oh so acutely still alive.

You made a hell of a mistake, he thought. Only the mistake had been leaving her, instead of staying.

He reached out, hands trembling, and drew the box towards him. Although the night was pleasantly warm the wood felt cold, incredibly cold, but that coldness came from within him.

A small padlock secured the box latch. He reached down, drew the Bowie knife from his boot sheath. Jamming it between the lock and latch, he pried, twisted, his vise-grip on the hilt making his hand bleach and his forearm ache. The lock was cheap, designed merely to hold the box closed, not prevent someone determined to break in from doing so. It snapped, a thin sound that might as well have been the thunder of a gunshot as far as he was concerned. He stared at the box for dragging moments, before returning the knife to its sheath.

Open it! a voice inside taunted.

No, another returned.

If he opened that box there was no going back, and any guilt he'd experienced over the last two years would be nothing compared to the regret that was coming.

Hand still quaking, he reached for his whiskey glass. With a sudden jerky motion he brought the glass to his lips and downed the remainder of the brown liquor; it burned its way down his throat, but did nothing to quell the Black Norther surging through his being.

He slammed the glass down, drawing a few looks from bargirls and cowboys. With a deep breath, he snatched the broken lock from the box, flung it onto the table.

Open it, the voice inside entreated again.

No, please . . . please don't make me. . . .

As if the box were a coffin, he lifted the lid.

What happened beyond that point became a surging blur of images and emotion. The storm of darkness inside raged up, completely overwhelming his senses, his judgment, his self-control. Through hazy consciousness, streams of horror-bathed guilt, regret, self-recrimination, he heard a scream of agony rip from his very soul. The sound cascaded past his lips, utterly without restraint, and he bolted to his feet. The box lid slammed shut with a sound like a clap of thunder, echoed in his ears and in the shredded essence of his sanity.

All other sound in the bar room ceased. Folks stared, gawked, their eyes wide, their mouths agape, their faces frozen in shock at the sight of a man who'd kept to himself for the past week, a man who'd demanded his solitude, now suddenly going stark raving mad for no immediately discernible reason.

But he had a reason, didn't he? A goddamned good one.

Waves of emotion – guilt, pain, fury – roared through him. His hand swept out, flinging the whiskey bottle from the table. It rebounded from the bar that ran along the east wall, rolled to a stop a half-dozen feet away.

He jammed his hands to either side of his head, wanting to crush the tremendous grief and the sight of what lay nested in the box from his brain.

A stench, the putrid sharpness of decomposing flesh, had touched his nostrils for only a moment, but it sent waves of nausea through his belly and surges of bile into his throat. He doubled over, vomited onto the sawdust-covered floorboards.

Folks had come from their seats by now, were

moving away from him, faces still aghast, eyes filled with fear.

Every muscle quaking, legs rubbery, he straightened, blood-red fury sweeping across his vision. The room appeared coated with a scarlet film and every stunned face became a threatening mask. Inarticulate shouts babbling from his lips, he staggered forward, arms sweeping out, hurling bottles and glasses from tables. Tears streaked from his pale-gray eyes and scarlet faces blurred.

'*What have you done?*' he screamed, falling against a table, leaning heavily against it for support. 'What the hell have you done?'

His mind unhinged, careened through the past, images of men he had killed flashing, followed by images of the woman he'd loved, who'd meant more than life to him, and glimpses of another man, a man with a wild beard and wilder eyes.

Another agonized scream tore from his soul.

'I'll kill you! I'll kill you all!'

Without a shred of control or compunction, his hand swept for the Peacemaker at his hip. In that instant he couldn't have controlled his actions; he would empty its chambers into whoever stood in front of him, guilty or innocent, because each face was that of a man he now despised with all he was and ever would be. A man responsible for an act so heinous and cruel it could not even be considered remotely human.

A man who was going to die over and over again.

You can't do this . . . some remaining fragment of humanity begged him. *It isn't their fault. . . .*

No, it was *his* fault, *his* responsibility. *He* had caused this by making two decisions long ago that had led to this moment: in a moment of weakness he'd refused to kill a man and in another he'd made an excuse to leave the woman he'd loved.

Those points had now converged, horrifyingly.

That hesitation, that dissenting voice, might have been the only thing that prevented a once-good man from committing an atrocity.

Something crashed into the back of his head. He staggered forward, away from the table, hand slipping from the ivory grip his Peacemaker.

Whirling, he nearly lost his balance and went over sideways, barely managed to keep his feet. The bargirl whom he'd sent away a few minutes before stood there, fright on her face, the whisky bottle he'd flung gripped in her hand. She'd hit him with it, the thought penetrated his rage-filled mind.

'Damn you!' he yelled, not at her but at a man who years ago had sworn revenge on him and put into motion his retreat from Serena's life. That man had somehow located him, somehow escaped or been released from prison. 'Damn you, Markello!'

The bargirl uttered a startled bleat and swung the bottle. He saw it coming but was damned if he could get out of the way. It thudded against his skull and blackness swarmed from the corners of his mind.

His knees folded, despite a gallant effort to stay upright, and he went down, the side of his face slamming against the floor.

Horrified murmurs thrummed all around him; a sea of blurry faces swam before his eyes.

Then blackness cycloned and he knew nothing more.

CHAPTER THREE

The darkness swam with images. Faces swirled up, one, a woman's, with flowing auburn hair and a tender smile that melted everything frozen inside of a man named Logan Priest. At times he swore her touch penetrated the cold shadows imprisoning his mind; he felt every sensation, every emotion as her fingertips traced the swirls of hair on his chest and her lips fluttered across his skin. The taste of her kiss lingered and the rhythm of her heart against his drummed like a gentle rain as they lay together in the blackness of her room at the ranch house. Her windchime laugh filled his senses, caressed his soul.

For a spell he was no longer a man who gunned down vicious killers, no longer a force of justice who hunted the guilty and hanged them from a convenient cottonwood or dragged them battered and bleeding back to the law.

No longer a callous man without compassion or an empty future.

Serena was back and with him now, and they would always be together. Everything would be all right.

But then blood streaked down her soft face, obliterating her porcelain features. Her flesh melted away, leaving only a grinning skull. That skull dropped to a sawdust-covered floor and rolled towards him, its black sockets staring, accusing, damning.

You let me die. . . .

Her voice, one moment lilting, the next shuddery, hollow. Dead.

Another laugh replaced Serena's, a man's, a monster's, harsh and drenched with mockery. Another face rose in the blackness, one with a wild beard and wilder eyes, the reflection of the Devil within them.

'I promised I'd done break you one day, Priest,' the grinning face said. 'I promised you and it's just begun. Find me, Priest. The way I found you and the way I done found her. Find me and surrender your will. . . .'

With the outlaw's taunting words the blackness dissolved and hazy light filtered in, stinging his eyes and making his head pound. He glimpsed another image, another face, blurry, unreal almost, a woman's, her long blonde hair cascading over her shoulders and blue-gray eyes luminous as they looked upon him with concern.

Then gone. Blackness swarmed back for an indeterminable time, and he drifted in a sea of guilt, pain and horror, craving only the desire to perish and escape the guilt.

A scream tore from his lips and he sat bolt upright in a bed. Light flooded his vision and he pressed his eyes shut against the glare. His heart thundered and every god-awful emotion he'd experienced in the bar room raged back in shuddering waves.

'I'll kill you!' he shouted. 'Damn you, Markello!'

Something pressed against his chest and he was too weak to resist. 'Shhh,' a soft voice came and he felt himself pushed back down; his head sank into the pillow.

With a great pounding in his skull, blackness returned. He wasn't sure for how long he wandered, lost, within it. It felt momentary, but could not have been, for when the light came back it was buttery, softer, unlike daylight. A lamp burning on a small table beside the bed, he determined, opening his eyes for an instant, before pressing them closed again until they could adjust to the glare. A lamp meant night had fallen and he had been out for at least a few hours.

No, that couldn't be right, could it? He recalled intermediate glimpses of daylight, so at least twenty-four hours had passed, likely more, because he recollected glimpsing blurry sunlight numerous times.

This time, however, he woke less abruptly, without a scream or his heart thundering. Still, his skull throbbed, though at a lower level than as on the previous time he'd regained consciousness.

He licked his lips, which felt incredibly dry; his tongue and throat were parched.

'Here,' a gentle voice said, and he opened his eyes, this time able to keep them so. A young woman held a glass before him; it was half-filled with water from a pitcher that rested near the lamp upon the small table next to the bed. She tipped it to his lips and he drank, some of the water trickling down either side of his face. She returned the glass to the table, then with a cloth dabbed the corners of his mouth.

She was lovely, with long blonde hair tumbling over her shoulders and luminous blue-gray eyes that reflected glints of lamplight. Full of bosom and soft of feature, she might have been some sort of angel and he would have wondered if perhaps he had died, if not for the fact he was certain anyone greeting him on the other side would be of a more hellish persuasion. Vague recollection came to him; he'd glimpsed her on the previous time he'd woken; she was the woman who'd pushed him back to the bed.

'Hey,' she said, a small smile flickering across her lips.

'How . . . how long?' he asked, struggling to lift

his head, but it felt filled with lead and he let it sink back into the pillow. The effort commenced a throbbing thunder in his skull.

'Two weeks, goin' on,' she said.

He pressed his eyes shut again, wishing he had not woken, that he'd simply remained in that world of black grief and guilt in which he had been trapped, and had never emerged. Because when awake the memories tormented him all the more; they slashed at his being with claws of accusation and condemnation. In a rush of emotion he remembered everything: the bar, the box, *Markello*.

'Where am I?' he asked through gritted teeth. He swallowed against the burning emotion balling in his throat.

'Room back of the doc's,' she answered, taking the cloth and wetting a corner, then dabbing his forehead. 'Some men from the bar brought you in. The bargirl hit you pretty hard with that bottle, but I reckon it was more than that. Doc thought maybe you wouldn't wake up again, that maybe after what happened you wouldn't want to. I told him you would. I told him a man like you had to.'

He nodded, the motion paining his head and neck. His eyes roved, gaze taking in the peeling *fleur-de-lis* wallpaper and sparse furnishings. Moonlight bled through an open window and a soft breeze wafted in.

'You should have let me die,' he said, reproach

36

sharpening his tone.

Her eyes widened a fraction. 'No, Mr Priest, I could not rightly do that. Won't let anyone die under my care again.'

'Again?' His gaze focused on her. A flash of pain crossed her eyes.

'It's not important right now, Mr Priest.'

'Reckon it ain't.' He studied her soft features. In a way, she reminded him of Serena; they both had a certain kindness and compassion that radiated from within. 'Who are you? I think . . . I think I saw you in town once or twice. You were new here, too.'

She nodded. 'Didn't rightly think you noticed me. I've been working for the doc the past three weeks. I came in 'bout the same time you did. My name's Dawn, Dawn Hawthorne.'

'You know who I am?'

A frown creased her lips and sadness darkened her features. She looked away, as if pondering her answer, then back to him. 'I know. Lots of folks recollect who you are still. You used to be a big name in these parts.'

'One folk too many,' he said, voice bitter. 'But I ain't nobody. Not anymore.'

She shook her head. 'You're somebody, Mr Priest. You're somebody dangerous.'

A humorless laugh trickled from his lips. 'I used to be. . . .'

She peered at him, face hardening. 'No, not used

to be, Mr Priest. You're *more* dangerous now. I can see it in your eyes. You just ain't realized it quite yet, but you will shortly. Something happened in that bar room, something that's going to change what you've been for a spell. You've become someone . . . something else.'

He wanted to laugh it off, but a chilling coldness suddenly flowing through his innards told him she was dead right. Something had changed. It was as if he had been rewired, self-pity turned into a craving for vengeance, guilt forged into a desire for a reckoning. He would not go back to drinking a half-bottle of whiskey each night in some unknown bar room, wallowing in despair and helplessness. He had become the man he had been two years ago, yet at the same time, something else, something entirely more deadly and determined. Something inhuman, perhaps, like a machine driven only by the need for retribution.

'What was in that box, Mr Priest?' she asked, her face tense, yet still compassionate.

He jolted, then pressed his eyes shut, a sight, blood-red and horror-drenched, flashing across his mind. Opening them again, he looked at her. 'My life. . . .'

She shook her head, seemingly taken aback by the chilled look that must have reflected from his pale gray eyes.

'I don't understand. . . .' she said.

'It's best you don't.'

She lowered her head, placed the cloth back on the table. 'I have a confession to make. Truth is, Mr Priest, I knew who you were because I came looking for you.'

'How did you know where to find me?' He reckoned there was too damn much of that going around for anyone's good.

'T'weren't hard. You're still known, though to be blunt some folks figure you for a joke now.'

He nodded, the pain in his skull less this time. 'I'm aware of my reputation, leastwise what it's become. Otherwise some owlhoot would've put a bullet in me by now.'

'Reckon that ain't it.' She frowned. 'Reckon they treat you as a joke but know better than to test that theory. I got a notion most of them are still afeared of you.'

'Reckon I'm an easy mark, just the same, if they were smart enough to think it out.'

'Only 'cause you choose to make yourself such by spending your time drinkin' away a memory. . . .' Her gaze drilled into his and he wondered how the hell she was able to read him so well.

She uttered a gentle laugh. 'I know guilt when I see it, Mr Priest. I know hurt and I know loneliness and losing something you hold dear. You aren't so very hard to figure. But I also know you weren't going to do nothin' about it, either, least not until you saw whatever came in that box.'

'Leave me the hell alone!' he snapped, annoyance pricking him for no reason he could figure other than the fact he didn't rightly care for a stranger sifting through his thoughts. Serena used to be able to read him that way, and it made something in his gut cinch.

She ignored his tone with a small chuckle. 'I ain't scared none of you, Mr Priest. I reckon others would be but you ain't the monster you figure yourself for. I can tell that, too. You're a kind man, least you were once, to those you cared about.'

'How the hell do you know a damn thing about me?' He turned his gaze from her, her probing eyes making him uncomfortable.

'I don't, Mr Priest, least other than the things I've read and heard. But I know people. I know good people and I know bad people. And I know people who got so much pain inside they can't go on with their lives. People who feel so much guilt they can't live with it and they can't live without it.'

He turned back to her. 'Yeah? What makes you so damn good at readin' folks that way?'

'Because I'm one of them, Mr Priest. I'm one of those people. And I can't live my life unless something gets taken care of. I s'pect you'll be going forward that way, too.'

'I ask you again, who are you, Miss Hawthorne? Who are you really and just what the hell do you want from me?'

'Right now, I want you to recover.' She folded her arms across her full bosom. 'Truth is, I wanted to talk to you that first week you rode in. I asked around a bunch of towns in line to this one, discovered you'd visited a handful of them and figured this might be next on your list. I was right. I saw you the day I came in. My husband . . . he left me a horse. And some money.'

'You used past tense . . . your husband . . . he leave or—' His voice came gruff, and at once he wanted her to leave him be yet stay beside him.

'He left this world, and not by choice, Mr Priest.' She hesitated and sadness brought tears to her eyes, but she held them back. Her lips quivered, but only for a heartbeat. 'I wanted to talk to you but you seemed . . . unapproachable. Been tryin' to figure a way. Saloon ain't partial to allowing women inside other than of a certain type, and I am not one of them.'

A humorless laugh escaped his lips. 'And you figure an opportunity presented itself with me laying here flat on my back?'

'No . . . not like this. I just offered the doc help, trying to make a little money while I was here; I used to do some nursin'.' Her eyes narrowed on him and muscles tightened in her jaw. 'I was waiting outside the saloon that day, waiting for you to come out. I determined myself to talk to you then, but something happened. I heard screams. When I looked in I saw you close the box and saw the awful look on your face. I saw you go insane and I saw the bargirl hit you with the bottle. I ran and got the marshal and the doc.'

'Whatever you were aimin' to say I reckon it don't matter. You were right, I got other business to attend to now.' He tried to lift his torso from the bed but a burst of dizziness made the room swim.

'Easy,' Dawn said, gently pressing her hands to his chest and forcing him back down. He fell back, for the moment too weak to resist. He reckoned he hadn't eaten in two weeks, though she and the doc had probably forced some water into him or he would have been dead.

'You best get your strength back,' she continued, tone softening.

'Soon as I do, I aim to see a man dead.' His words came almost a whisper, coldness swarming through him again. It was with utter disconnection that he imagined putting a bullet into a man, not simply to kill him but to make him suffer. Then another, perhaps in some vital yet not instantly fatal spot. While Logan watched, taking pleasure in that man's slow dyin', exacting every morsel of agony and horror that man had forced him to endure.

Dawn's face drained a shade and he knew she had glimpsed that frozen anticipation in his eyes. But to her credit she held her voice steady and did not draw back from him.

'I reckon you do. See, Mr Priest, your business and mine, they've crossed paths. Like I said, I know what you are—'

'Were,' he corrected with venom.

'*Are*,' she insisted, shaking her head. 'I know what you are and I know what you aim to do. I know you hunt down men the law can't or won't touch and that many of those men you hunt they don't come back living.'

'I'm not that man anymore.'

She laughed. 'Aren't you? Perhaps two weeks ago you weren't, Mr Priest. But now . . . now you're that and more, least as far as one man is concerned. And that's right fine by my thinkin', 'cause I want a man dead, as well.'

He eyed her, puzzled, annoyed, yet unable to deny a flicker of interest. Perhaps had the situation been different he would have given more of a damn.

'Like I said, I got other business.'

Her gaze didn't waver. 'And like *I* said, your business and mine, they've crossed paths.'

'You figure.'

'I do. Because I aimed to talk to you about a man, Mr Priest. A man you brought to justice, years ago. An evil man. An evil man who murdered my husband.'

He couldn't deny a measure of sympathy, but he

forced it away. Her problems were her own and his life had one purpose, one focus, then it was over. 'I ain't interested. I just want to get out of here.'

'You *are* interested, Mr Priest. Leastways, you will be when you hear this man's name.'

'I doubt it, Miss Hawthorne. Right now there's only one fella on my list and after that—' He was about to say he would end his life, but refrained. He didn't need to tell her that, though that was certainly his plan. After he took down that man, there was no point in going on. Without Serena, his life held no meaning and he was damned if he was going to spend the rest of his days living with the guilt of her blood on his hands.

'You don't understand, Mr Priest. I'll pass it off as the blow to your head and being mostly unconsciousness for the past couple weeks.'

'Please, just leave me be. . . .' The words came low, because somewhere inside he *did* understand. He just didn't want to acknowledge that a mistake he'd made had caused even more pain, not to a woman such as this, one who reminded him of Serena.

'I didn't see what was in that box, Mr Priest. But when the marshal took it out I saw the initials on it.'

Something plunged in his belly, confirming what he already knew. 'This man . . . you want me to go after . . . his name. . . .'

She turned away, a tear streaking down her cheek.

She whispered a name, a name that had been branded onto his very soul.

Markello.

CHAPTER FOUR

It took Logan Priest another five days before he felt strong enough to climb out of bed and pull on his trousers. Sitting on the edge of the mattress, his face in his palms, his soul felt heavy and his emotions had become a barren, ice-glazed landscape where pain and regret lay boiling just beneath the surface, waiting to erupt at the first hint of a crack. But he couldn't let that happen. He had too much to atone for, too many mistakes and sins for which to answer. His biggest error, not putting a bullet in Markello years back instead of bringing him in, had resulted in the death of the very person he'd sought to protect by leaving. And until that death was avenged, he refused to allow himself the luxury of unbridled grief.

Mistakes. They came back to haunt a body and this one . . . this one had returned like a vengeful spirit.

Living without Serena, that had been a choice to

46

this point. For him, at any rate. Now ... now Markello had stripped him of that option.

Serena was dead. Murdered. And it was his fault.

You shouldn't have left her. . . .

Forcing the thought away, afraid to dwell on it, he sighed. His head lifted from his hands and bright morning sunlight streaming through the small window in the back room at the doc's office stung his eyes. He'd waited until Dawn had left on an errand for the sawbones before climbing out of bed. Her fawning over him made him uncomfortable, reminded him too much of Serena and the way she used to minister to him when he was ill.

Dawn Hawthorne had made no bones about wanting him to resume his manhunting role to track down Markello for murdering her husband. Her request was unnecessary, because nothing on God's green would have prevented him from going after the killer, but with her request came an unspoken appeal. He could read it in her eyes. She wanted to accompany him on that quest, wanted to witness Markello's death.

And that was simply out of the question. There was no place for a woman in what he planned to do. He'd failed to protect one already; he wouldn't have another's blood on his hands.

As soon as he settled with the livery man for boarding his horse and gathered his saddlebags and bedroll from his hotel room, he would be on his way

47

and never see the young woman again. It was better that way. For him; for her; for everyone. The news of Markello's death would surely get back to her some way. He wasn't exactly unknown in these parts.

Logan recollected with bitterness the frustration and nagging worry that had coursed through his veins the day Markello had escaped a hangman's noose via a fancy frocked-coated eastern lawyer.

Logan hadn't anticipated that. He had fully expected Markello to hang for his crimes and that had played into his decision to bring the outlaw to justice. Problem was, most of the evidence against the outlaw consisted of hearsay and rumor; Markello had been accused of heinous crimes, wholesale slaughter of innocent families, but had left little in the way of proof behind. He had a peculiar following of misfits, led them around almost as if they were under some sort of spell. A few had accused Markello of being the Devil himself, claimed that somehow the outlaw's wild eyes reached into a body and bent its will to his own.

Logan had seen those eyes, and damned if he could dispute the claim. Something *was* different about that man, as if he'd been born without a soul and the emptiness left had been replaced by pure black evil.

You should have killed him. . . .

So many folks had wanted to see Markello hang. At the time Logan brought him down he figured denying them that satisfaction would have been wrong. Those folks who had lost loved ones, they deserved to see Markello put down. But it hadn't worked out that way, had it? Markello had avoided a hangman's noose. Maybe the outlaw did have some peculiar control over a man's will. Or maybe someone in the system that tried him had been corrupt. Whatever the cause, Logan accepted all responsibility for the mistake and vowed it would not happen again.

He's waiting for you, somewhere . . . watching.

Markello had been stalking him for a spell, that much was obvious. And somehow he had traced a trail back to Serena.

Searing grief burned in his belly and emotion tightened his throat. Tears welled in his eyes but he refused to let them flow. He forced the anguish down, letting the chilled numbness of vengeance settle back over him. He had no time for emotion; there was an avenger's work to be done.

With the thought, the old rush of adrenaline and fire in his veins he'd felt as a manhunter on the trail started to return. His skills would be rusty, his wiry frame weakened by too much whiskey and self-loathing, but he reckoned he had enough left to put a bullet in Markello. Although he wasn't a big man, just a shade past five-feet-eight, he was tough as rawhide. He used to be lightning with a Peacemaker; that would need some work, he reckoned, but he could practice on the trail.

He pulled on his boots and slid his Bowie knife into its boot sheath. Standing, he grabbed his shirt from a high-backed chair and shrugged into it, feeling every muscle complain with the stiffness of being in a bed for too long. A dull ache throbbed in his lower back and a low pounding permeated his skull. He fought off a moment of dizziness, steadying himself with a deep breath.

The sound of a scuffing boot drew his attention to the doorway and his gaze swept in that direction. A lawman, arms folded, a grim expression pinching his face, leaned against the jamb. The lawdog, an older man, had iron hair, mutton-chop sideburns and a chimney-sweep mustache peppered with gray.

'Figured I'd be gettin' a visit from the local law sooner or later,' Logan said, voice firm. 'Was expectin' it 'fore now.'

'Miss Hawthorne told me you weren't ready for visitors, but I got tired of waitin'.'

Logan nodded. 'You here to arrest me?' He grabbed his gunbelt from the back of the chair, buckled it on. He didn't want any trouble with the lawman but wasn't about to be held in this town any longer than need be, either.

The marshal, whose name was Helfner, stepped into the room, doffed his hat and frowned.

'No, reckon I ain't got nothin' to arrest you for. You didn't kill anyone and . . . well, I rightly can't fault a man for going a bit loco after what I saw when I opened that box.'

Logan nodded, swallowing hard. 'You know who she is – *was* – by now, I figure. . . .'

The marshal nodded. 'Sheriff over in Barlington's a friend of mine. Discovered her body at her ranch, minus . . . well, minus what was in that box. He was pretty shaken up over it. Said she never made no trouble for no one. Everybody in town was friendly with her.'

Logan uttered a small sound clotted with emotion. 'She never had a cross word for anyone, Marshal. Serena Hedison was a hell of a woman.'

'You knew her intimately, I take it. . . .' It wasn't a question but Logan nodded anyway.

'Damn near married her. Left her because I thought she'd be safer.' A bitter laugh trickled from his lips and the marshal's eyes glittered with sympathy.

'But it didn't turn out that way.'

'No, reckon it didn't.'

'You couldn't have known. . . .' A note of solace came in the marshal's voice but it was lost on Logan.

'You're wrong, Marshal. I could have. I should have known and I'll spend the last of my days torturing myself over it.'

'Who would do such a thing, Mr Priest?' The marshal's brow lifted as Logan cast him a mildly surprised look. 'Oh, yes, I know who you are. Many

51

folks hereabouts still recollect Logan Priest. You were once the greatest manhunter who ever lived, I hear tell.'

'That were true Serena Hedison wouldn't be dead.'

'Can't stop them all, Mr Priest. You save some, lose others.'

'Why is it we lose those who matter most to us?' Bitterness invaded his tone. Although the marshal was right, he had indeed saved untold lives by his success in bringing down some of the animals, but in the end he had forfeited the person he cared about most.

The marshal shrugged. 'Sometimes we're too busy savin' the world to save our backyard.'

Logan ran a hand through his brown hair, sighed. 'Is it worth it, Marshal? Is it worth losing someone you love to save folks you don't know from Adam?'

The lawdog's eyes narrowed and he worried the edge of his hat. 'I'd like to think so. Course, I might think different if I lost someone I care about. I can't blame you for the way you feel now.'

'I got plenty of blame for myself, I reckon.'

The lawman studied Logan and Logan turned to the window, stared out into the sunlit street.

'You got a notion who did it, who killed her?' the marshal asked.

Logan turned back to the man, face washing white, pale-gray eyes glittering with hate.

'I got more than a notion. You see those initials on the box?'

The lawman nodded. 'DM. I have an idea who that might be. You weren't the only one famous around these parts a few years back.'

'Demarte Markello.' Logan said the name with spite, the taste of it acrid on his tongue. 'I put him away a few years back. He swore revenge. Pretty typical scenario, far as owlhoots go. Few of them ever make good on it. Mostly air.'

'Not this time, if'n it was him.'

'It was him. This man . . . this man had a wildness in his eyes and a deadness in his soul. He was capable of anything. Day I brought him in I truly thought he would hang for his crimes. But he didn't and I left Serena, because I knew he, or someone like him, would be a threat to her.'

'Seems to me you should have stayed. You could have protected her better.'

Logan uttered a mocking laugh. 'Don't have to tell me that, Marshal. The same thought's run through my head a hundred times the past week.'

'Assuming it was him, you planning on just shooting him in cold blood?'

Logan didn't answer. He didn't have to. It was plain in his eyes.

The marshal sighed and set his hat back on his head. 'There's no denying the initials on that box and an obvious connection. Markello's s'posed to be in a cell, but word has it he escaped a short time back. Sheriff in Barlington asked around and a few folks reported catching sight of a man answering to his description near your woman's ranch. Said the stranger had questioned a few folks about you, asked about anyone who might know where you went, whether you had any relations or friends in the area. Apparently they inadvertently pointed him Serena Hedison's way and Markello, for as much of a bastard as he was reputed to be, isn't a stupid man.'

So that was how Markello had made the connection. So damnably simple.

'Anyone see where he went?'

'Well, that's the question, now, isn't it?' The marshal frowned. 'One of Markello's old gang members was trying to start a new life, go straight. Turned up dead in Blazeville, a couple towns over.'

'He's making it easy for me.'

'How so?'

'Darkton. His old haunt. Barlington, Blazeville, this town, nice straight line pointing to Darkton. He wanted me to know it was him and he wants me to come after him, or he would have just killed me by now. I would have been an easy enough target.'

'Men such as him got their arrogance, I'll give them that. But you sure even Markello is capable of such a thing? Cutting off a woman's head and sending it to you in a box?'

'Reckon that don't require an answer, Marshal.

Fact of it speaks to it he is. All that's left now is revenge.'

The marshal's brow furrowed. 'Careful, Mr Priest. Vengeance ain't always ours to dispense, and it leaves a stain on your soul.'

Logan uttered a thin laugh. 'I got no soul to stain any longer, Marshal. Markello took it from me.'

The marshal sighed and turned to walk out of the room, then paused in the doorway, his back to Logan. 'I took the liberty of sending her head back to be buried with her body.'

Logan swallowed hard. 'Much obliged, Marshal.'

'I don't have to tell you, Mr Priest . . . in all my years as marshal . . . most gruesome cruel thing I ever saw. . . .'

Tears flooded Logan's eyes again, but he held them back and didn't answer. He turned to stare out into the street, losing himself within the incredible coldness inside his being.

A half-hour later Logan Priest walked out of the sawbones's office, his legs unsteady but regaining strength quickly. Bright sunlight glinted from windows and sparkled from water troughs. Folks wandered along the boardwalks of the wide main street, as if nothing heinous had occurred, the memory of it likely forgotten since there had been no follow-up strikes at the citizenry.

They could count themselves lucky there.

Markello usually took a notion to stay around, invest his time in recruiting a few followers, but Logan supposed the outlaw was aiming at only one thing this time – vengeance on the man who had put him away.

He recollected most of Markello's followers had been rounded up, a few hanged, with the rest rotting in cells for smaller crimes. They hadn't been lucky enough to afford fancy eastern lawyers, so had been punished accordingly.

Searching his mind, he came up with a name from that time, that of one of Markello's group who had gone free. A young woman who looked more like a boy, named Mousy because she had dirty gray-brown hair cropped as if she had taken a Bowie knife to it.

Would Markello contact her? Would the former gang member be in Darkton?

Mousy, if Logan recollected right, liked to spend time in saloons, passing herself off as a man to get into those that forbade women who didn't work the line. Once he reached Darkton, Logan aimed to look her up, if she were there. Markello had left an easy trail, too easy, and likely that was a trap, part of the outlaw's game plan. Logan would need to counter that, somehow, and perhaps Mousy was a way to strike first.

Logan drew a deep breath; the air was warm, smelled of horse dung and dirt. Something about being back on the trail of a killer felt almost – was comfortable the word he was looking for? At least he had a direction and right now that was what he needed. If he had to sit around wallowing in his thoughts any longer he didn't think he would be able to stop himself from going insane.

Had the outlaw kept tabs on him the past few weeks? The marshal hadn't said anything about Markello being spotted anywhere in town. But surely the killer had some way of keeping an eye on the situation, especially since he'd gone to so much trouble to leave Logan alive instead of murdering him outright. Logan considered checking with the boy who'd delivered the box, but his manhunter's intuition told him that would be a waste of time. Markello had left enough in the way of tracks, letting himself be seen in those other towns, killing one of the few of his old followers not dead or in jail. The boy would be able to tell him nothing he didn't already know or suspect.

That left riding to Darkton, by way of Barlington.

'I'm going with you,' a woman's voice came from behind him, snapping him from his thoughts.

He turned to see Dawn Hawthorne, a package cradled in her arms, peering at him intently, determination on her face. In the sunlight she looked even lovelier and something inside him cinched, coming with a flash of memory of Serena riding in the dawn light, her auburn hair ablaze with gold and her eyes filled with life. Feeling his legs go weak, he quickly forced the image from his mind.

'The hell you are.' His tone came intentionally harsh, but he would not risk this woman's life by letting her accompany him when he went after Markello. He would protect her from the killer, whether she wanted it or not.

The way you protected Serena by leaving her?

The thought stung and he shook his head, started to turn away, having no desire to discuss it further.

'Don't turn away from me, Mr Priest.' She took a step towards him, her lips drawing into a grim line.

He peered back at her, sighed. 'Look, miss, I'm not intending to be unkind. Truly I'm not. I'll find this man and I'll finish what I should have years ago. But you aren't going with me.'

She stiffened. 'Markello killed my husband. I aim to see him pay for that.'

'He *will* pay for it.' He wondered why he was even bothering to argue with her about it. He should have just walked away, but something about her blue-gray eyes compelled him to explain himself. 'But you don't need to be there. You'd just slow me down.'

'I can ride as good as any man, Mr Priest. I wouldn't slow you down—' She hesitated, studying him. 'But that ain't it, is it? You ain't really worried about me slowing you down. You're worried about me getting killed.'

He wished she'd stop prying into his thoughts; it was damned annoying. 'Don't know what you're talking about, miss.' The lie was obvious. He'd never been particularly good at hiding the truth.

'I ran into Marshal Helfner at the general store. Said he had talked to you. Told me what was in that box, too, who she was.'

He gazed down at the worn boardwalk, struggling to suppress the emotion threatening to crumble his inner shell of ice. That shell was too thin, too brittle, and he knew it. It wouldn't take much to send him over the edge again.

'Don't see how that is any of your concern.'

A sympathetic look filtered into her eyes. 'Perhaps it isn't, Mr Priest. Perhaps it isn't. But I know you must have cared about her powerfully or you wouldn't have reacted the way you did in the saloon. I also got me a notion you left her, a long time ago, maybe. And that maybe you wanted to protect her by staying away from her.'

'You suppose too damn much.' His tone hardened, but she would have none of it. Her chin came forward.

'Keeping away from her didn't help, did it, Mr Priest? I ain't aimin' to be mean, just truthful.'

'What the devil you gettin' at, Miss Hawthorne?'

'Dawn. Call me Dawn.'

'Call me Mr Priest.'

A flicker of anger crossed her eyes. 'You can't

protect folks by leaving them to themselves, *Mr Priest*. I reckon you know that by now, or will figure it out pretty soon. And I don't need your protectin'.'

'Choice isn't yours.' He staggered under a wave of emotion, then. The sudden biting recollection of himself saying those very words to Serena two years ago made his belly cinch and his heart hammer.

She saw it in his pale eyes too, read his thoughts as if he'd written them on paper. 'I want to see that man die for what he did. He's a beast, Mr Priest. An animal. His eyes . . . I ain't never seen nothin' like them. . . .'

'You saw him?' Surprise overcame some of the emotion tearing at him.

'That ain't important, now, is it? All that matters is finding him and me going with you.'

'I'm going alone,' he insisted, but his words had no effect he could note. She was determined and that meant he was going to have to sneak out of town without her. 'That's that,' he added, turning and starting down the boardwalk.

'Is it?' she called after him. 'You're cold inside now, Mr Priest. But once you find him . . . are you goin' to be able to hold onto that? You won't be able to stop your rage and he'll have the advantage. He's like that, I hear tell. He controls people and he's already got you half in his power because he knows what hurts you. I can help you, Mr Priest. Ain't nothin' colder than a woman whose loved one's been taken.'

He wished to hell she'd shut up, because a niggling voice of dread deep in his mind taunted him that she might well be right. Everything inside was frozen now; for the moment he was a chilled, impersonal machine bent on vengeance. But grief, rage, all seethed just below the surface, waiting to burst free. When he saw Markello, how would he react? Coldly, as he planned, able to put a bullet in him? Or would those emotions explode and leave him vulnerable?

The fact he could not answer the question should have given him more pause. But it didn't. Which made it plain to him that he was still a damned fool.

An hour after dusk Logan Priest gathered his saddle-bags and bedroll and slipped out of the hotel. All day, Dawn Hawthorne's words had troubled him, but no more so than the very vision of her in his mind. He reckoned it was because she reminded him so much of Serena and the way that the young woman used to read him. Whatever the case, he would not risk her life by allowing her to accompany him and that was indeed that.

You didn't protect Serena by leaving her. . . .

He stuttered slightly in his step with the thought. No, he hadn't, but that was different, wasn't it? Logan wasn't positive just how Dawn had seen Markello, or whether the outlaw had seen her.

Didn't seem likely a man like that would have left her alive were that the case, but if she had escaped him somehow, bringing her along would make her an open target. There was little doubt in his mind Markello would strike at her first, the way he had at Serena. While planning and scheming had never been Markello's strong suit, at this juncture the killer held most of the cards. Logan refused to allow mistakes this time, refused to take risks with another's life.

He went to the livery stable and saddled his mount, a chestnut, then led the animal out into the darkened street. Shadows cloistered everywhere, broken only by the buttery light cast from hanging lanterns or fire glow bleeding through a window. Laughter and curses, yips and yowls came from the saloon a bit down the street. Everything had returned to normal for the revelers. But not for Logan Priest. For him, nothing would ever be normal again.

A few minutes later he rode out, as the moon climbed over the horizon and glazed the trail with alabaster. He had one stop to make, he reckoned, and though it was out of his way a bit, it was necessary. He owed her at least that much.

He traveled in silence, the occasional cries of night creatures sounding from the hills that rose to the left of him or the sparse forest that flanked the right. He hadn't been on the trail at night for quite a spell, yet something about it felt immediately comfortable. Strangely, he felt no need of whiskey, his mind too focused on Markello, his innards too chilled to consider drinking at the moment.

Two hours later found him on the outskirts of Barlington, where the land had opened into rolling fields of moonlight-glazed pasture. He drew up, his gaze beneath his hat focusing on the small dark shape of a ranch house in the distance. No smoke swirled from its chimney; no fire burned within its hearth. No life existed there, not any longer.

A single tear escaped his eye, trickled down his face. He heeled his chestnut into a slow walk, reining to a halt again a few hundred yards on, as he spotted a small wooden cross driven into the soil.

With a deep breath, he dismounted. His legs shook as he approached the cross.

How can you be gone?

He sank to his knees, his bleary gaze centering on the name on the marker: Serena Hedison. Another tear wandered down his face and for dragging moments the ice that had become his soul melted and burning grief took over. With trembling hand he reached out, touched her name on the cross.

'I'm sorry. . . .' he whispered. 'I'm so powerful sorry . . . I was trying to stop this from happening. I swear to God I was.'

A yell of rage suddenly tore from his being and he threw his head back, unable to stop the fury thundering through him. Lost in the terrible anguish and emptiness, he wasn't sure how much time passed.

Then a sound, behind him, that of another horse, penetrated his consciousness. Still, he could not even turn, so paralyzed was he by grief. If Markello had followed him Logan Priest was now a dead man and would have no chance at vengeance.

But it wasn't Markello. Because a moment later arms encircled his shoulders and he glimpsed blonde hair glazed by moonlight. The woman drew his head to her breast and held him.

'Christ, I told you—'

'Shhh. . . .' she whispered, and he said nothing more, merely surrendered to his pain and to her arms.

CHAPTER FIVE

Before sunrise Logan Priest and Dawn Hawthorne
saddled up and headed back onto the trail. They'd
ridden half the night, Logan needing to put as
much distance between himself and Serena
Hedison's ranch as possible before setting up camp
by an off-trail stream.

He might have blamed the young woman's having
followed him so easily on rustiness, two years of
whiskey and self-pity, but it had been more than
that. He'd been too preoccupied. As much as he
wanted to keep his emotions frozen, he had failed.

He glanced at the young woman, who sat atop a
bright bay, her doe eyes focused on the trail ahead.
Sunlight, just now peeking above the trees flanking
the right of the trail glossed her blonde locks, which
she'd pulled back into a ponytail. She wore a tan
blouse and a riding skirt with buckshot sewn into the
hem, and he could tell she was used to being in the
saddle.

'You want to ask me something?' she said, startling him a bit.

'Wish you'd stay out of my head,' he muttered, fixing his own gaze on the sun-ribboned trail ahead.

'Didn't have to get into your head, Mr Priest. It was plain on your face. Best say what you got to say and get it out of the way. But it won't change the outcome any.'

He knew she was right, but he said it anyway: 'Turn your horse around and ride back where you came from. Let me deal with Markello.'

She uttered a small laugh. 'You really expect that to happen?'

He had to admit he didn't but didn't want to give her the satisfaction of being right. 'Yes.'

She shot him a glance, one eyebrow arching. 'Really, Mr Priest, you're a terrible liar.'

She was right about that, too. 'You followed me from town?'

She nodded, focusing ahead. 'Wasn't hard. You were lost in your head most of the time. I reckon that's enough to get most manhunters buried.'

He nodded, forgetting to be contrary. 'Reckon it is. But it'll get you killed as well, and I don't want that on my conscience. I got enough there already.'

'You fret too much, Mr Priest. I make my own choices. You don't make them for me. Besides, you need me to watch your back. Markello would have come up on you the way I did . . . well, reckon we wouldn't be havin' this conversation.'

A prickle of irritation went through his nerves. 'You think you got me all figured out, don't you?'

She glanced at him, smiled wryly. 'Mostly.' A strange hitch came in her voice.

'What's that mean? What else is there to figure?'

She looked at him longer, steadier, her lips pursing and he could see thoughts passing behind her blue-gray eyes. She was struggling to find the words to say whatever was on her mind.

'Mr Priest, right now you're a man bent on vengeance, way I'm a woman fixin' on it. But there's a difference between us. I want to go on livin'. . . .'

He went silent, finding himself little interested in discussing that with her. He wished she would just turn her damn mount around and go back to where she'd come from, but from the determination on her features he knew there was no chance of that. At the same time, something about having her beside him made him feel . . . he wasn't certain. Perhaps somehow less alone in his mission.

Is there something more?

No.

It occurred to him a dissenting voice answered too abruptly, too definitively, but after a moment he shrugged it off, having no wish to visit that thought, either.

They rode on, three hours passing before the trail began to open and lead into low hills and rolling swales. A half-hour more found the sun beating down on his bibshirt like the Devil's hellfire. Sweat trickled from under his arms and beneath his hat. A few hundred yards beyond lay Darkton, a rambling town of clapboard buildings, seedy saloons and crooked streets. The place appeared built with no rhyme or reason and he reckoned that suited a man of Markello's mentality perfectly.

Was Markello there? Waiting for him? Where? Hiding? Or would the killer come right out into the open and challenge him?

No, Markello had some warped plan, one that involved Logan suffering, and it was not merely because Logan had put him away. It was because Logan Priest had been one of the few men Markello had had no power over at the time, was unable exert his force of will upon.

Anyone in the past who'd resisted the outlaw, Logan reckoned, wound up with a bullet in their hide. Markello was a man who thrived on breaking the wills of others, turning them into helpless sheep to do his bidding. Half the reason Markello had escaped hanging was because the crimes for which the court had evidence could only be traced back to a follower's blood-stained hands, not the outlaw's.

But, as Logan had noted, Markello was not normally a man for plans or strategy. Perhaps in some way the outlaw had changed, but a man's basic nature never strayed far for long. Was that something Logan could employ to his advantage?

He was going to need a strategy, the way his manhunter skills had eroded.

He drew up at the outskirts of town, surveying the twisting main street. A few folks scurried about the boardwalks and everything appeared relatively peaceful. If Markello was awaiting him, he was not doing it in the open.

'What's wrong?' Dawn asked, drawing up beside him.

He shook his head. 'Nothing yet, I reckon. Everything looks calm enough, for this town. Darkton's long been known to harbor unsavory types.'

'You certain this is where he will be?'

He nodded, frowned. 'I'm certain. He left breadcrumbs. He wants me to find him.'

'Then let's get on with it.' Her face tightened and he saw hate and pain wash into her eyes.

'We best be careful. There's a hotel down a ways.' He reached into a pocket, dug out a roll of greenbacks. After peeling off a few bills, he passed them to her and returned the roll to his pocket. 'Go in first by yourself and get us two rooms. I ain't totally sure Markello doesn't know who you are. He scouted me for a while, so he might have done the same before killing your husband.'

She studied him, as if seeking to determine whether he was merely trying to get rid of her. 'All right, Mr Priest. But like I said, I don't need protectin' and I'm not letting you leave without me.'

He almost smiled, the first easy emotion he'd experienced in perhaps years. 'I figured as much.'

She gigged her horse into a trot and headed for the town. He rested a forearm on the saddle horn and waited until she reached the hotel, then gave it another fifteen minutes.

He would need a place to start and if Markello were here perhaps Mousy would be as well. It was still early in the day, but from the foot traffic he noted one saloon open for business. Logan would start there. If the outlaw's follower wasn't within, perhaps the barkeep's tongue could be loosened with a double eagle or two.

Logan heeled his horse into motion and headed for the saloon. His gaze roved, alert. He searched rooftops for any glints of sunlight off steel, but he doubted lurking as a sniper would be Markello's style, not after going to the trouble he had to set Logan on his trail.

He drew up and dismounted, then tethered his chestnut to the hitchrail. With a deep breath, he stepped onto the boardwalk, finding himself a bit more jittery than he expected.

After pushing through the batwings, he paused on the landing overlooking the bar room proper, surveying the interior. A handful of men occupied two of the dozen tables. A few whores with belladonna-glazed eyes sat about, looking apathetic and uninterested in any within the room. A couple gave him a lascivious lick of the lips or bat of the eyelashes, but it was more comical than seductive, in his estimation.

His gaze halted on a form perched on a stool, narrow shoulders hunched over the bar. A hat rested on the bartop and Logan noted the brown-gray cropped hair, and something in his belly twisted. He fought against a surge of rage, knowing if the sight of that person could do this to him he might be in trouble indeed when he encountered Markello.

But with this one it didn't matter, did it? With this one he could turn his fury to his advantage.

He took the three steps down to the bar room proper and headed for the figure, certain it was Markello's right-hand follower, the one named Mousy. The figure swung upon hearing his bootfalls and Logan saw her face then, boyish and haggard, barely discernible as a female, and marked by years of cheap whiskey and laudanum.

A startled look crossed her face and he figured even if she had been expecting him she hadn't been expecting him right this moment.

She tried to slide sideways off the stool but he reached her first. He grabbed a handful of her shirt, lifted her off the stool and hurled her over a table. She let out a muffled groan as she hit the floor and rolled.

The barkeep and two other patrons flashed him threatening looks, came half out of their chairs.

It came back to him then, the one skill he'd always had, the speed of the draw. His hand swept downward to the Peacemaker at his hip as if no time had passed. He drew it in a blurred, fluid motion, swung it up and around, aiming at the barkeep's chest.

'Don't!' he ordered, knowing the man might go for a shotgun or some other weapon beneath the bar. The barkeep jerked up both hands and backed up a step. The two others settled back into their seats, apparently wanting no part of this man whose gray eyes glinted with ice and whose face was a mask of violent intent.

Logan swung the gun, just as Mousy was trying to get back to her feet.

'Stay down,' he said, thumbing back the hammer.

She gazed up at him, spite and viciousness in her dull, brown eyes.

'What you want?' Her voice was husky, and with her lack of hip and bosom it was damned hard to tell she wasn't a man.

'Reckon you know exactly what I'm here for. Or should I say "who" I'm here for?'

It got a reaction but not the one he expected. The outlaw girl started to laugh, a braying sound that rode his nerves.

'Whatever the hell you talkin' about, pistol boy?'

she asked, eyes narrowing.

'Markello, where is he?'

Her laugh got louder and he had to suppress the urge to knock her in the teeth with the gun.

'You best ask the marshal that, Priest.'

'What the hell are you talkin' about?'

She shook her head, laughed again. 'Go see the marshal. He can tell ya exactly where Markello is.'

He was tempted to pound the answer out of the girl, but refrained. While he was certain she was nearly as vicious as Markello, a restraining sense of chivalry held him back.

'Take your gun out, slowlike,' he said. 'Set it on the floor beside you.'

She eyed him defiantly, but complied. Once she had placed the weapon on the floor he kicked it. It went twirling across the room and settled in a corner, where she wouldn't be able to make a quick grab for it.

'You don't go anywhere. Marshal doesn't tell me what I want to know I'll be back and it won't matter to me a lick you're a girl.'

She didn't respond, merely held his gaze, something not quite right, not entirely rational staring back at him.

He backed to the steps, then up to the batwings, not taking his gaze off anyone until he was out on the boardwalk.

Once outside, he holstered his Peacemaker and

surveyed the street, spotting the marshal's office.

He untethered his horse and walked the chestnut along the street towards the office. A few folks gave him passing glances, but made no move towards him. He fought to suppress the rage rushing through his veins, finally getting himself under control as he reached the marshal's. After tethering his mount, he stepped onto the boardwalk.

Going to the office door, he paused, taking a deep breath. For an instant a memory flashed across his mind. No, not so much a memory, but more a vision, one of Serena standing in the field outside her ranch, waving goodbye. The vision swirled with gray mist and sadness radiated from her face.

This is wrong. . . .

Her soft voice echoed through his mind. Serena had never really approved of his profession, at least the killing part. She had seen that as pure vengeance and told him it was something that corrupted a man's soul. She had understood the choices he made, but wanted him to stop, settle down, and maybe a small selfish part of him that had needed to do what he did, needed to put down men who preyed on others, had played into his decision to leave. He had wanted to stop, hadn't reckoned he could, because he had become addicted to manhunting as if to a drug. He had convinced himself in the absolute that what he did was right, was necessary, though there were times when he could admit he should have brought more men in to the law officers than he had; sometimes a bullet was just easier.

The ironic thing was, he thought with bitter comprehension, that the very thing he had done to hold onto his addiction had resulted in its demise, at least until now. For in leaving Serena, any desire to continue in his manhunting role, his duty, had deserted him. Self-pity and shackling introspection had removed the craving for justice. The addiction, as it turned out, had not been justice; it had been her. And now, sober in more ways than he wanted to be, he knew that understanding had come too late.

He shook from his thoughts, his hand clamped about the office door handle, aching. The vision of her in the misty field dissolved, leaving only gray ice and grim determination inside him.

Serena was wrong about what he was doing now not being right. Killing Markello would be an act of righteousness. A man like that was a danger to every innocent person and gunning him down needed no justification, even had the slightest morsel of remorse surfaced in his mind.

It struck him, though, that for Dawn Hawthorne it would indeed be wrong. She was unstained by the darkness that often simmered beneath the surface of a manhunter's makeup. She was driven by the craving for justice where her husband's death was concerned, but she had no blood on her hands.

Witnessing the outlaw's death would do her no good in the long run, though she had convinced herself it would provide a modicum of satisfaction in the short.

There were nights in his nightmares when even he saw the faces of those he had killed. He didn't want Markello's dying image haunting her. What that monster had done to her life would do that enough already.

He hadn't been able to stop her from accompanying him, but he could still dispose of Markello without her.

He drew another deep breath and entered the marshal's office.

The chill inside him suddenly dissolved and became a raging inferno. For across the office, sitting in one of three cells that flanked the back wall, was the very man he had come to kill.

CHAPTER SIX

Logan's hand shook with rage as it started towards his Peacemaker.

'Don't even think about it, Mr Priest!' a voice boomed from beside him, accompanied by the *skritching* of a hammer.

Logan's hand stopped in mid-draw. Muscles to either side of his jaw bunched as he felt the cold steel of a gun barrel suddenly against his head.

This time it hadn't been rust that had dulled his manhunting skills; it had been unbridled fury at the sight of Demarte Markello sitting on the edge of the bunk in the middle cell. The outlaw's wild eyes rose to meet Logan's and even enraged Logan felt the compelling power within those dark orbs reach out for him. But he refused to take a step back.

Markello turned over a watch in his hand and grinned.

'Pony show's set to begin,' Markello said, voice low, laced with mockery. 'Why so shocked, Priest?

You expected me to be here in Darkton, didn't you? I sure hope you did.'

Markello hadn't changed a bit. Logan clearly recollected the feral eyes and beard, the very presence of evil that clung to the man like a dark cloud.

'Relax your hand, Mr Priest,' came the voice beside him again. 'And we'll talk this all out nice and gentlemanly-like. Won't ask again.'

Logan felt the Peacemaker plucked from its holster and turned his head to see a marshal standing beside him. The marshal was a young man but heavy lines branched from his mouth and eyes. Dark half-circles nested beneath them. Logan sized the man up immediately; he'd seen enough such lawmen in his days, ones on the take, looking out only for their own interests. This man was one of that breed, crooked as a bow-legged horse and likely had his hand in the tills of any number of the town's illicit enterprises. The question was, why did he have Markello in a cell?

'You know who I am, Marshal,' Logan said, not a question.

The lawdog nodded. 'Marshal Gabe Weathers. I know. Saw you coming across the street and recognized you. I reckon lucky for my prisoner I did or I might be arresting you for murder.'

'Wouldn't be murder, Marshal. Would be a mercy killing.'

'For who, Mr Priest?'

'For any number of folks whose lives it might save.'

'Sit down, Mr Priest.' The marshal withdrew the gun from Logan's temple and motioned with it towards a hard-backed chair in front of his desk. Logan, his initial fury at seeing Markello becoming a strange dead numbness within him, went to the chair and sat. He saw little other choice at the moment.

The marshal went around to the back of his desk and lowered himself into a worn leather chair, still holding onto Logan's gun. He opened a drawer, with a thumb spun the cylinder and emptied the Peacemaker of bullets, then shoved the drawer closed. He slid the gun across the desk to Logan. Logan took it, holstered it, knowing he couldn't reload in time to avoid a bullet from the lawdog's own weapon, which the man kept ready in his hand.

In his cell, Markello's wild eyes focused on Logan and the grin on his lips didn't change. He turned the pocket watch over and over in his hand, a peculiar nervous trait Logan recalled from the trial a few years back. At one point, church goers attending the trial claimed the man's very gaze was enough to stop their own timepieces from functioning and that Markello's was the only one left working, proving it to be the Devil's very own timepiece.

'You didn't think you could just walk in here and gun down a man in cold blood, did you, Mr Priest?' The marshal's gaze pinned him, challenging, almost . . . Logan wasn't certain, but it looked as if the lawman were vaguely satisfied about something.

'Fact of the matter is, him being here was a complete surprise, Marshal, but I would surely have killed him where he sits.'

'Why's that, Mr Priest? And to answer your earlier question, I am well aware of who you . . . were.'

'That man killed—' Emotion clutched in Logan's throat. 'He murdered a woman in Barlington, and a man a few towns over.'

The marshal uttered a choppy laugh. 'Reckon that's right impossible, Mr Priest. See, I arrested Mr Markello for robbery a few months back. Town council tried and found him guilty and he's been sitting here in my jail ever since. So you see, he couldn't have murdered anyone.'

Logan's gaze shifted from Markello, a chill shuddering through him. He probed the lawdog's eyes; the marshal had clearly imbibed something. His eyes were webbed with crimson, the pupils dilated.

'Reckon you're a liar, Marshal.'

That got a reaction, but only a flash of one. 'I don't take kindly to being called such, Mr Priest, even by a famous man such as your own self.'

'I don't take kindly to folks protecting murderers,

Marshal Weathers.'

A harsh laugh came from the cell, and Logan's gaze swung back to Markello.

'Done got unlucky, gettin' my ass caught robbin' that store. I been here all along, Priest. Just a'sittin' playing with my watch and waitin' for the time to pass.'

Logan had prided himself once on being able to read when a man was telling the truth, though obviously those skills were rusty. But with Markello ... Logan simply saw no flicker of emotion or telltale sign the man was lying. Even years back, when he'd brought him in and Markello claimed he hadn't killed any of those of whose death he had been accused, Logan hadn't been able to tell. It was as if the man had no soul, no delineation between right and wrong, between a lie and the truth.

Rage started to flow again in Logan's veins but he struggled to keep it in check. Markello had somehow been out of that cell, but for the moment the outlaw held the advantage with the lawman on his side.

Logan's gaze went back to the marshal. 'You got a good notion just who that man in your cell is?'

The lawdog nodded, a smug expression turning his lips. 'I know exactly who he is. Demarte Markello.'

'Then you know he escaped jail and is a wanted man. Why didn't you inform the country marshal?'

'Didn't see no need. What's the difference what cell he's sitting in as long as sitting in one he is?'

'The difference is I take him back and he hangs for two murders.'

The marshal let out a chiding laugh. 'Oh, come now, Mr Priest, we both know damn well if I let you take him he never makes it to the authorities. I reckon it'd be all you could do to leave the town's border before putting a bullet in his brain.'

No point in arguing that, because the marshal was dead right. Markello wasn't going back to any cell, ever. The only place he was going was in the ground.

Logan stood, every muscle in his body feeling as if fire ants were biting into his nerves. The very man he had come to exact vengeance upon was no more than twenty feet from him and he couldn't do a thing about it. Heat flushed his face and he slid his teeth together.

'I aim to see that man pay for his crimes, Marshal,' Logan said. 'You best not get in my way again.'

'Reckon I don't take well to threats, Mr Priest.' The marshal came from his chair, his hand tightening on his gun.

'I ain't making any,' Logan said, turning, his gait stiff as he went to the door. He gave Markello a glance, his pale-gray eyes glittering with ice chips.

'Your time's damn near up, Markello. I'll see you burn in hell for what you did.'

'I've done been to hell already, Priest.' Markello's wild eyes shimmered and again Logan felt as if some dark power radiated from them. 'I right liked it.'

Logan opened the door, stepped out, wondering if he would make it to the hotel before his sanity gave out.

'He gone?' Demarte Markello asked from the cell, as the marshal stared out the window into the sunlit street.

The lawdog glanced back at Markello, nodded. 'He went into the saloon. He was walking like a man on his last nerve.'

Markello laughed, tucked his watch into his vest pocket, and stood. He went to the cell door and pulled it open.

'Reckon that's right where I want him,' Markello said, coming up beside the marshal and peering out. The marshal shuddered, whatever dark force Markello possessed washing through him.

'You're takin' an awful chance with a man like that, ain't you?'

'A man like what, Weathers? A man who's been lost in a bottle for too long a spell? A man I left bleeding his soul out all over the place by sending him his woman's head? Logan Priest ain't half the man he once was and he got lucky the last time when he brought me in.'

'Or you did,' the marshal said, frowning.

Markello laughed a dark laugh, the wildness in his eyes like cornered wolverines. 'You got it all wrong. That man . . . that man who just left here . . . you'd have never got the drop on him two years ago. He's nothing anymore, and he'll be less once I done get finished with him.'

'You should just kill him and be done with it, then.'

'Reckon a few years back I would have done just that. But I had me a lot of time to think while sitting in that jail. Priest was the only man I didn't have no effect on and that just drives me plumb loco. I needed to know why. I needed to break him.'

'And you think you know now?'

Markello nodded, brow cinching. 'I know. I reckoned then he was a man with nothing to lose. But I was wrong and I figured it out. He was protectin' someone, someone he loved and she gave him strength. But once I took that away from him I was in. Now I'll finish it, destroy him before I kill him.'

'Still reckon you're poking a rattlesnake.' The marshal shook his head, avoided Markello's gaze as he returned to his desk.

Markello turned from the window and peered at him. 'Ain't your place to reckon, Weathers, only to follow my orders.'

The marshal squirmed under Markello's gaze, feeling the man's very will pry into him.

'Still say plannin' things ain't like you. You been awful antsy waitin' on him to come. Thought you might just go bursting out of here and kill him.'

Markello's eyes glazed over as if he were lost in some dark world, one filled with screams and blood and terror. The marshal could see the battle raging there; whatever controlled Markello's debatable sanity was dangerously close to shattering. The marshal had no desire to be around the man when that happened. No one, not even his followers would be safe from Markello's wanton bloodlust, then.

Markello's eyes settled to their normal wild stare. 'It's contrary to my ownself, you're right. But necessary. Priest is different. So I have to be different. Adapt. That's how I've survived all these years. By adapting.'

The marshal was inclined to disagree. He reckoned Markello had survived by rattlesnake meanness and his nearly hell-spawned ability to influence other men.

'What about that woman who rode in just before he did?' the marshal asked.

'I recognized her. She was Hawthorne's wife.' Markello looked back out the window, as if contemplating something, and the marshal was just as glad to have that devil gaze off him.

'You think she's with Priest, or is it just coincidence?'

'I don't rightly cotton to coincidence. She's with him. I reckon she's lookin' for revenge on me for killin' her man. I wondered where to hell she done got off to that day. Was downright disappointed I didn't get to kill her, but didn't figure she'd be a problem.'

'She might be—'

'Or perhaps an asset. . . .'

'How you figure?' The marshal shifted his own gaze to the street beyond the window.

'Ain't certain yet, but if she's with Priest he'll want to protect her. His kind always does.'

'A manhunter?' The marshal cocked an eyebrow. 'Thought they didn't rightly care much about collateral damage.'

'Not the manhunter kind. The moral kind. Priest is one of them. He ain't like regular bounty men. He don't do it out of need for money, he does it out of righteousness. I reckon he thought that he was dead inside till I sent him that box. But I saw it today. He's still alive in there. An' he won't be ready to die until he kills me. I'm sure that will be useful.'

'If he don't kill you outright, way he was aimin' to do a few minutes ago.'

Markello laughed a dark laugh, fished in a pocket and brought out a small gun. 'He wouldn't have got the chance. I was ready for him and the memory of his woman's death was too fresh for him to use his skill rationally. See, that's the goddamn problem with men who have souls . . . those souls jest get in the way.'

CHAPTER SEVEN

By the time Logan Priest walked into the saloon a stormy jumble of emotions plagued him – rage, grief, disgust, contempt for the crooked lawdog, hate – but none of them the icy composure he'd counted on protecting him from himself the moment he encountered Demarte Markello.

Emotion had crippled him. He would have gunned Markello down in his cell, but had the outlaw possessed a weapon and been ready for him the results might not have gone Logan's way. His own fury had caused him to stutter in his draw, hesitate. He could not afford that sloppiness against a man such as Markello.

You still sure it's him?

The marshal had told him that Markello had been in that cell the whole time, but Logan reckoned the lawman was worse than many of the crooked officials he had run into across the West. He was protecting a vicious killer and likely

Markello held some sway over him, the way he did his other followers.

Other followers. Logan wondered just how many might be embedded in this town; he doubted Mousy was the only one. That meant he couldn't afford careless mistakes. Markello being in that cell had caught him unawares, so he reckoned maybe that was some excuse, but not enough of one and it might still have gotten him killed.

Who gives a damn?

He'd asked himself that question a thousand times over the past couple years and at the moment all his self-pity and lassitude came rushing back. Serena was dead. Did revenge matter so much now? Maybe simply letting himself be shot down would be better. Maybe joining her was better than avenging her.

After he pushed through the batwings, his gaze swept the bar room. He had half a mind to corner Mousy and take his rage out on her, send a message to Markello, but the outlaw's follower was nowhere to be seen.

He went down the three steps to the bar room proper, a few cowboys casting a wary eye on him, as did the barkeep.

'We don't want trouble,' the 'keep said, as Logan reached the bar.

Logan gave him a mocking grunt. 'Should have thought of that before your town started harboring a killer.'

The barkeep's eyes narrowed and a pained look crossed his face. 'I don't want him here. None of us does.'

' 'Cept the marshal, I reckon.'

'Marshal . . . Marshal's on his own. We ain't got no say. He runs this town – least he did.'

Logan nodded. 'Until Markello came in.'

The bartender remained silent, but his expression confirmed Logan's words.

'When'd he come in?' Logan wondered if the man would try to lie. He saw fear in the fellow's eyes and fear was a powerful drug. 'And why ain't you under his control? Way I hear tell Markello's got a right powerful effect on folks.'

The barkeeper's eyes darted and Logan swore he saw him shudder. 'I first noticed him about three months back. Just saunterin' along the street like he owned the whole damn town the moment he walked into it. You see his eyes?'

Logan nodded, motioning at a whiskey bottle. The barkeep fetched it, passed it to him, and Logan clinked a double eagle onto the counter.

'I've seen 'em. Can't deny they're the Devil's own.'

The barkeep shuddered again. 'It's like the fellow ain't human or something. He has this power over folks. I didn't more than see him a couple times but I knew better'n to get in his way.'

'So he rode in and robbed a bank?' Logan said it

with a note of mockery.

'He rode in and started pallin' around with Marshal Weathers, like he knew him from some place.'

It was possible, Logan figured. Markello had to have a few stragglers out there besides Mousy.

'I never heared nothin' about him robbing a bank,' the 'keep continued.

Logan's brow arched. 'How long he been in that cell?'

'Can't say. Haven't seen Markello for weeks. Then rumor had it he was in a cell over to the marshal's. Couldn't figger out what the hell was goin' on.'

'That makes two of us.' Logan opened the bottle and took a swig. The liquor burned its way down his throat. The few weeks he had been without it had made a difference but it felt as comfortable as an old saddle. 'What about his little second, Mousy?'

'You know she's not a fella?' the barkeep's brow furrowed.

'She might as well be.'

'She's in here a lot. She's a drunk. Not sure why Markello would even keep her around.'

'Does what he tells her, I reckon, and I doubt she's got much compunction about what it involves.'

'She's a mean gal, that one. Wouldn't put nothin' past her.' The bartender hesitated, a plea washing into his gaze. 'You here to take him? Markello, I mean? Most folks in here want him gone soon as possible but no one dares lift a finger to make that happen.'

Logan uttered a small laugh. 'No, I ain't here to take him anywhere.' The barkeep's face fell and Logan gave him a thin smile. 'I'm here to put a bullet in him.'

He grabbed the bottle and went to a table. As he lowered himself onto a chair, a strange numbness washed over him. He took another swig of the whiskey. It was awful, bitter, poor stuff, yet welcomed. Three weeks ago he wouldn't have even noticed.

So what do you do now, Logan? That man's protected in a cell. . . .

The marshal was crooked but Logan couldn't just put a bullet in him the same way he intended to do with Markello. Markello was a diseased wild animal, deserving of his fate. The marshal might be a run-of-the-mill, bought-off criminal but the line between vengeance and murder was a thin one. He couldn't kill a man in cold blood for aiding and abetting at this juncture. He needed more evidence of complicity.

The batwings creaked open and he looked up to see Dawn Hawthorne standing on the landing. Her gaze settled on him and she frowned. She crossed the landing and came down the steps. After reaching his table, she pulled out a chair. The barkeep gave her a look, but didn't bother to stop her. Apparently she met with more approval than the other woman he'd catered to earlier.

She remained silent, studying him, and he felt his self-pity and anger soften a bit. Serena had always been able to do that to him, calm him whenever his innards raged. It was as if she had possessed some sort of spell the exact opposite of Markello's, one that was good, gentle, quelling.

'You plan on making yourself an easy target again, Mr Priest?' she said at last, disapproval lacing her tone.

'How's that?' He took a swig of the whiskey, thumped the bottle down.

'Back to drinking instead of finding your man, way you told me you planned. Drunk you would be a right easy target to shoot down, don't you think?'

'Already found him.'

Her eyes widened with shock. 'What? Where? He dead?' This time hope brightened her tone.

'No, not dead, not even close to it. He's in a cell at the marshal's. Marshal even says he's been there a spell, too long to have shot down your husband and killed . . . Serena.'

She shook her head, defiance in her blue-gray eyes. 'That ain't true and you know it. I saw him kill my husband.'

He stiffened, suddenly pushing the whiskey bottle away. Her eyes bled pain and tears welled but didn't flow.

'I never asked you the details, but I reckoned you must have come home to find your husband dead and seen Markello riding off or something to that effect.'

She shook her head again, shuddered, and wrapped her arms about her full bosom. 'Ain't the way it happened. My husband—' She hesitated, jaw tightening. 'My husband used to be one of Markello's followers.'

Logan's belly cinched. 'Reckon that explains what Marshal Helfner told me about a former gang member being found dead. I failed to connect it with your husband's passing, though.'

'Why would you? Do I look like the wife of a criminal, Mr Priest?'

He shook his head. 'No, reckon far from it.'

A flicker of a smile touched her lips. 'He went straight. Told me about his association with Markello after we married. He was always worried Markello would escape one day and come back.'

The revelation only added to Logan's guilt. If he had only killed Markello when he had the chance, instead of bringing him in. 'If you saw it happen, how is it you aren't dead?'

'My husband caught a glimpse of him riding in. He made me go to the root cellar, but I could still see everything through a crack in the floorboards. He threatened my husband, wanted him to rejoin. Said he was going to get a gang together after he took care of some personal business and that that business was murder.'

'I reckon he took care of it.' Bitterness laced Logan's tone.

She nodded, sympathy in her eyes now. 'I saw the whole thing. He—' She shuddered, face washing pale. 'He nearly cut off his head, Mr Priest. I can't get the sight of it out of my nightmares.'

'I'm sorry,' he said, in almost a whisper. 'How'd you know I was here at the saloon?' He wanted to change the subject, talk about anything that didn't force him to face the pain in her eyes because it reminded him far too much of his own.

'I was coming out of the hotel to look for you. I saw you come in here. Are you just going to drink away the day now that you can't get at him the way you planned? He give you that devil stare of his and send you away with your tail betwixt your legs?'

'That don't concern you.' His tone came harsher than he expected, but she was goading him and he knew it. He was in little mood to be pushed.

'Don't it? You want to get your ownself killed, I reckon I can't stop you, Mr Priest. But that man is going to pay for his crimes one way or the other.'

'Just what's that s'posed to mean?' He didn't like what he heard in her tone, the resolve that caused folks to act without thinking. He'd heard it in his own often enough to recognize it instantly.

She reached into her skirt pocket and pulled out

a derringer, set it before her on the table. 'You don't kill him, I will, Mr Priest.'

'Give me that damn thing,' he said, reaching for it. 'Before you get your sorry ass killed.'

She plucked the gun from the table, shoved it back into her pocket, then came out of her chair. Fire blazed in her eyes. 'I reckon I wasted my time countin' on you for help. You're just a drunk and a coward.'

She spun, stormed towards the batwings. The words stung more than he would have expected. He wasn't sure why he gave a damn what Dawn Hawthorne thought of him, but he did. As he watched her go, his blood boiled and emotion melted the remainder of the ice inside him. He struggled to hold onto his sanity, suppress the waves of grief and fury that threatened to rage up.

He leaned forward, buried his face in his hands. Judas Priest, what was wrong with him? What had he become? Bad decisions, maybe cowardice where Serena was concerned, and booze had eroded not only his manhunting skills but the man he was, or thought he had been.

She was just angry, he told himself. She was trying to goad him out of his mood, but what if she was right? What if he had become nothing more than a drunk and a coward, a coward who gave up on things the moment they became too complicated or overwhelming?

His head lifted and he noticed the barkeep eyeing him, the same accusation on his face as had been on Dawn Hawthorne's. As well as maybe a plea for help, for action against a man who was a monster.

He shoved the bottle away and stood, let out a curse. Markello had unnerved him far more than he should have let him. It was time to get hold of himself. If not for himself, then for that woman who'd just stormed out, before she managed to get herself killed. Because if there was one thing she had been serious about it was the fact that she planned to kill Markello herself if Logan didn't.

Just who does he think he is anyway? Dawn Hawthorne thought as she strode down the boardwalk, heels of her high-laced shoes clomping. Here he had found Markello and done nothing? And now he was in a bar room drinking his life away, making himself an easy target? And just when she thought. . . .

She shuddered, wishing she could deny it. Just when she thought she was starting to have feelings other than the hate and vengeance she'd been coddling over the past weeks. Feelings that maybe she could grow attached to that man once her husband's death was avenged.

It was a downright peculiar thing about the man she planned on avenging, her husband. She had thought he loved her when they wed, but that was never so. He was a man of different tastes and a marked past and he had told her so. He had told her six months into their matrimony he had married her to change his ways. Most of his ways, for there was one he did not change. Could not change. He had gone straight in a criminal respect and had no wish to return to what he had been under Markello's influence. But in another respect. . . .

She had caught him sneaking out many a night to be with 'others' and though it sickened her she had reckoned marriage was a commitment a woman made forever, no matter what. She had been foolish. Despite his preferences, he had never treated her unkindly and she had fostered the notion he might come to love her one day, that she could change him. That day had never come but in his last moments he had protected her, spared her from what would have been certain death the day Markello came to their ranch. He had sacrificed himself to keep her alive. She owed him something for that. Owed him justice and peace and she was a woman of her word, whether that promise was to herself or to another.

She wondered now if she had ever truly loved the man she married. She reckoned she had, at least at first, but knowing about his tendencies, that he preferred his own kind . . . that had changed things. No, perhaps that wasn't what had changed her emotions. She might have lived with that, because he couldn't be expected to be someone he wasn't inside. No, it was knowing he would never love her and her alone, never fully commit to her, that had altered their relationship.

Her love had withered in the end, but her honor had not. She would kill Markello and avenge her husband's death if Logan Priest failed to do so.

She sighed, slowing her pace. She regretted the things she had said to the manhunter, now that she was starting to calm. She had only been trying to make him realize what he was doing to himself but maybe she had gone about it the wrong way. Some men weren't meant to be pushed. Maybe Priest was one of them. But she couldn't allow him to get himself killed.

Her gaze settled on the marshal's office across the street and she half-considered bursting in there and killing Markello herself. But the marshal would likely gun her down first. She could hit what she aimed for but was no match for a lawman and a bigger gun. Even if she wounded Markello she would end up dead. But maybe it would be worth it to rid the world of that monster.

The choice was suddenly taken from her.

Deep in thought, she had crossed in front of an alley and as she stared towards the lawdog's office she failed to notice two men sidling up to her until one of them grabbed both her arms from behind. Both attackers wore hoods and the second man, the smaller of the two, clamped a filthy hand over her mouth before she could scream.

She kicked backward at the shins of the man holding her, missing. He shoved his arms beneath her breasts, then dragged her backward into the alley.

The man holding a thin hand across her mouth suddenly pulled it away but before she could let out a sound he backed-handed her and her senses spun. Pain lanced her teeth and her legs wobbled.

'Should have stayed where you belong, Missy,' a voice came from the smaller man and though the tone was husky enough to belong to a young boy, she swore the voice was feminine.

The smaller attacker doubled a fist and hit her again and she collapsed to her knees. The man holding her let her sink.

With her last remaining willpower and consciousness, she jabbed her hand into her skirt, clasped the derringer. Jerking it free, she tried to swing it towards the smaller man but he saw her clumsy move coming. He kicked her in side of the face and the gun flew from her grip.

'Kill her!' the small man said, looking to his bigger partner, eyes darting beneath the cutouts in the hood.

CHAPTER EIGHT

That fool woman was going to get herself killed, thought Logan as he shoved through the batwings and stepped out into the bright sunlight. While he was willing to risk his own hide by feeling sorry for himself and drinking away his chance at vengeance he was not willing to risk the young woman's life.

Christ almighty, she had been right anyway, no matter how much it irked him. He had let Markello get to him and nearly thrown away any chance at bringing peace to Serena's memory.

It occurred to him there might be another emotion wheedling its way into the back of his mind, but he quickly dismissed such a foolish notion. He'd grown a mite attached to Dawn Hawthorne merely because she reminded him so much of Serena, but going after her to prevent her from making a stupid move and getting herself killed was something he would have done for anyone.

That's what he kept telling himself, anyway, as he

strode down the boardwalk in the direction of the marshal's office.

He wondered why he didn't see the young woman on the boardwalk, heading in that direction herself. Could she have already reached the marshal's office?

His heart stepped up a beat. He sure as hell hoped not because if she had that meant he was too late.

Maybe she hadn't gone there, he told himself. Maybe she had returned to the hotel instead. He would have liked to believe that but couldn't shake the odd premonition of doom washing over him – that manhunter's sixth sense coming back. Something felt . . . wrong.

He paused, gaze searching the street in the direction of the hotel, but still he saw no sign of her.

In his estimation, she could not have reached the hotel yet, and that notion only strengthened the dark dread brewing in his innards. Markello's second hadn't been in the bar room . . . could she have intercepted Dawn? Did Markello have others in town? Had the outlaw seen her that day he killed her husband, or perhaps in scouting the home beforehand? Had the marshal or Markello seen her ride in earlier today?

Muscles tensed in his hands, but he took a deep breath and forced himself to relax. A tense manhunter was usually a dead one. His fingers drifted to the handle of his Peacemaker as he started forward again, this time his senses alert, eyes scanning every nook and cranny of the crooked street.

It's funny how easy it was coming back to him, his manhunting skills, the caution, now that his head was a little more clear and worry over the young woman sharpened his nerves. Nothing distracted him now, the way it had when he visited Serena's grave or encountered Markello in the marshal's office. He wasn't numb or frozen inside any longer, either. He was just. . . .

Ready? Maybe that was the right word. As if he had slipped into a familiar groove, gained a focus. Maybe he had the young woman to thank for that, but first he had to find her, because everything inside him was screaming that she was in some kind of trouble.

His steps gained speed, and he hopped off the boardwalk to prevent his boots from clomping on the boards. Scanning the street, he saw few folks about, none of them seeming the least bit interested in his business.

A sound, a snapped order.

He paused, barely catching it above the clamor of his own heart and pulse throbbing at his temples. The voice was harsh, high like a young boy's, and had come from somewhere just ahead.

He spotted an alley and his lips tightened into a

hard line. The voice came again and this time he heard it more distinctly, recognized it: Mousy, and the words: 'Kill her!'

Logan's heart jumped into his throat, pounding, and his blood rushed. He launched forward, hand still on his Peacemaker, ready to draw.

Don't lose another one. . . .

He forced the thought from his mind, letting instinct take over, drive him. This time he wouldn't freeze and he wouldn't be stopped by a crooked lawman.

Reaching the alley, he pressed flat against the side of a store wall, then peered around the corner.

In a glance, he took in every detail: two men, both hooded. The smaller of the two he felt certain was Markello's second, Mousy. Dawn was on her knees, reeling as if she'd been hit, and he noted blood trickling from her lip. A bigger man stood over her, his hand going for a Bowie knife at his waist.

Logan acted without thought, without hesitation. Whatever skills he had remaining guided him.

He spun into the alley, hand a blur as he drew his gun.

The smaller hooded figure spotted him, suddenly bolted for the opposite end of the alley.

The larger man's hand hesitated on the hilt of the Bowie knife, preparatory to drawing it, as if he were debating running after his partner. If so, he made the wrong decision. He whisked the knife from its sheath, and in nearly the same move tried to sweep it back and lop Dawn's head from her shoulders.

Logan triggered a shot.

He had relied a bit too much on his speed and two years of whiskey and trail rust affected his aim. The bullet, intended for dead center of the man's chest, punched into the attacker's shoulder instead.

The shot, however, achieved its goal, stopping the man from taking off Dawn's head. The impact kicked him backward, the knife still in motion. Dawn had enough of her wits about her to pitch forward with the sound of the blast and the blade whisked over her head.

The would-be killer staggered a step, blood gushing from the shoulder wound. He spun on Logan, tried to hurl the knife.

The Bowie whipped through the air and Logan went to his right. The blade, missing, thudded into the store wall.

The hooded man froze. 'You gonna shoot me down in cold blood, Priest?' he asked, voice harsh, one Logan didn't recognize.

Logan's gun came up, centered on the attacker's chest. His finger hesitated on the trigger. He wanted to pull it, but now that the man was unarmed, the situation was a little different. He had a choice again: take the man in or deliver his own justice for attempted murder. The hooded attacker had probably killed others. Logan knew it, but since he couldn't see his face or know his history, that was mere supposition. Could he kill a man based on that alone?

If you bring him to the marshal, he'll be out on the street again within hours. . . .

The notion pricked him. The marshal wouldn't hold the man on Logan or Dawn's word, not if he were in league with Markello.

Logan's gaze drifted towards Dawn, who was trying to push herself back up to her feet, then went to her derringer lying in the dirt a few feet from the would-be killer.

'I let you live and take you in, you'll be on the street in no time,' Logan said, his pale-gray eyes narrowing on the man, who stood rigid. 'Just your attempt on her life tells me Markello knows who she is and wants her dead. I can't have that. I won't risk another innocent life.'

'Christ almighty, you just can't shoot me!' The man's voice suddenly quavered and he backed up a step.

'Way you couldn't just kill that young woman?' Logan paused, coldness washing over him. 'You get a sporting chance. See that derringer in the dirt behind you?' Logan nudged his head towards the little gun and the man looked back, his eyes darting beneath the hood. He looked forward again, then nodded.

'I see it.'

'Pick it up,' Logan said, his tone hard, brooking no argument.

'You can't be serious; I got no chance with that peashooter.'

'You got more chance than you gave that young woman there.' Logan ducked his chin at Dawn.

The man must have reckoned he had no choice because he suddenly dived for the derringer.

Logan let him get to it, grip it, come up and swing around. He had meant it when he said he would give him a sporting chance, albeit a fractional one.

The man aimed and pulled the trigger. Logan fired a split second earlier. The derringer issued a loud pop, but the man's gun hand jerked up as he stumbled backward, a .45 caliber slug punching into his chest.

The derringer bullet buried itself in the wall of the store. The hooded attacker crashed to the ground flat on his back, chest pumping scarlet, and lay still.

Logan holstered his gun, went to Dawn and offered her a hand.

'You all right?' he asked as she reached her feet.

She nodded. 'I'm alive.'

'Markello knows you're here and who you are, it's a sure bet. I misjudged him again. Just dumb luck and timing things didn't turn out worse this time.'

Again she nodded. 'Reckon that ruins any

advantage I had on him.'

'Maybe you won't need it. I thought about what you said. You were right. I ain't letting self-pity get in the way again.'

She looked into his eyes and an overwhelming relief that she hadn't been seriously hurt washed over him. He reached up, gently brushed a trickle of blood from her lips. Then he went to the gunman and grabbed the hood, whisked it off. The man's face was battered, weather-beaten, a typical owlhoot, but one whom he did not recognize.

He stared at the man a moment, then shoved his hands under the outlaw's arms, hoisted him over a shoulder and came to his feet. The man was dead weight, a good 200 pounds, but Logan was surprised at just how much of the trail strength was still in his wiry frame.

'What are you doing?' Dawn asked, after he started from the alley.

'Marshal's getting a special delivery package.'

'But won't he just try to arrest you for killing the man?' He glanced at her and her face was pale. The killing had affected her, and he hoped she thought long and hard about that.

'He can try. . . .'

Demarte Markello recollected a time when the days were soaked in scarlet and the nights were bathed in blood. He lay on the bunk in his cell, a crimson mist sweeping across his vision, enveloping his mind.

A small cabin, nestled in the forest. Four men, himself leading, Mousy riding second, galloping along the trail leading to his old homestead.

Dying sunlight cast a ruby glaze over the stony grounds and the cabin's pitched board roof covered with sod. Smoke curled from the chimney, gauzy crimson.

Blood fever raged through his veins, murder opium.

A roar cascaded from his throat as the fever surged and the last shreds of his control fell away. Chilled fall air whipped at his face and wild beard, snapped at his duster. His dark eyes flamed with wildness.

Blood. There would be so much blood. Running between his fingers, bathing his very soul. How he loved the gunmetal scent, the cool silkiness of it upon his skin.

How he loved killing, butchering. As much as he loved controlling men, bending them to his will.

The people in that cabin . . . they deserved what was coming. They had cast him out all those years ago, set him free in a world unwilling or unable to accept what he was, what he was growing into. He'd been barely 15, but his pa had caught him torturing a horse, and it was not the first time.

Evil, his own family called him, but he did not consider himself such. He was a visionary. He cut the fat from the lean, plucked the weak from the herd. Someday . . . someday the world would be ready for him. Some day the world would condone his vision.

He despised those in the cabin. Oh, so powerfully. Despised them as he had never despised any other he had murdered. This was personal. This would be liberating. He'd promised them he would return, and when he had been cast off he had seen that very fear lurking within his father's eyes. The old man knew his son would come back one day, and that it would certainly be the death of him.

And today, today that prophecy would come to pass. For he was Death on a horse.

They thundered up to the small house, reined to a halt. The front door burst open and he saw the old man, then, savored the look of terror that splashed across his worn saddle of a face.

'Christ Almighty, no—' the old man whispered, then tried to spin back into the house.

'Ain't hardly,' Markello said, leaping from his mount, then taking the distance to the porch in a single bound. The three riding with him followed suit.

Demarte knew his pa possessed but one weapon, an old Spencer, and he would not give him a chance to fetch it. He doubted the old man had the balls to kill his only son anyway.

He jammed a palm against the door before it could close in his face and shoved. The door and the old man flew inward. The old man hit the floor, flat on his back. Terror widened his eyes further and his lips moved but no sound came out.

Markello stopped just inside the door. How well he recollected the small parlor with its puncheon floor and battered tables and threadbare sofa. Recollected it with contempt, with hatred.

Within him, the blood fever raged stronger, and his head whirled and thundered with screams, voices shouting at him to wreak his vengeance, destroy those who had cast him out.

In a corner, his sister and mother cowered, terror stark reflections on their faces. He almost laughed.

His hand went to the Bowie knife at his waist and plucked it free. The hilt, full and cold in his grip, empowered him.

'Done told you I'd be back one day, old man,' he said, voice low, eyes glittering with madness.

The old man shook his head. 'There was always something wrong with you, boy. You weren't right in the head. I'm sorry for that. I truly am.'

'Don't be,' Markello said. 'I ain't never given it a moment of thought. I like it too much.'

'Please – please don't hurt your mother and sister – just take me.'

Markello uttered a strained laugh, gaze flicking to the women, then back to his pa. 'Honor . . . sacrifice . . . I despise those traits, old man. Only one that ever mattered to me was loyalty and it's clear you had none when you cast me out 'stead of accepting me for what I was.'

'But you were a monster—'

Markello smiled. 'I still am.'

The next moments became lost in a scarlet whirl of images and screams. Dying shrieks and pleas for mercy, all falling upon unsympathetic ears. His own gibbering laughter, like that of someone possessed, stabbed out.

It was over far too quickly.

Markello jerked upright on his bunk, a small sound escaping his lips. Sweat trickled from his forehead and streaked down his face. His breath beat out, and his heart thundered.

'What the hell's wrong with you?' the marshal's voice came.

Markello's wild gaze lifted, focused on the man sitting in the chair behind the desk. 'Nothing,' he mumbled, standing, legs shaky with the memory, the blood lust. The need to kill clawed through his nerves.

'Don't look like nothing,' the marshal said.

Markello shook his head. 'Reckon you were right. Sittin' here in this cell is done makin' me stir crazy.'

'You were always stir crazy.'

Markello's eyes narrowed on the marshal and the lawman tensed visibly, fear galloping into his eyes. 'Best watch that mouth of yourn.'

'Was your notion to pull Priest apart slowly and pretend to be sitting in a cell. Told you just to kill him and be over with it.'

Markello stared at the man, considering killing him, satisfying some of the bloodlust running through his veins. He might have done it had the door not burst open.

Logan Priest kicked the door open and stepped into the marshal's office, the body of Dawn's attacker slung over his shoulder.

This time he reckoned the marshal might be caught unaware and he intended to deliver the killer as a challenge to Markello. The outlaw had never been one for well-laid plans, so Logan figured maybe it was time to push him and see how long his new-found religion lasted. He was willing to wager not long.

Logan strode across the office, flung the body atop the marshal's desk.

For a moment the lawman was too stunned to move. His mouth dropped open and his eyes widened. 'What the hell?' he said at last, but made no move to get up.

Logan considered pulling his Peacemaker and swinging on Markello, then, but he noted the outlaw was up, his hand in a pocket. It wasn't much of a leap to figure Markello had a gun of some sort and as fast as Logan was, he couldn't take the chance a bullet from Markello might hit Dawn, who stood behind him, her gaze riveted to the outlaw. Her eyes flashed hate and he reckoned it was lucky at that point she'd forgotten her derringer in the alley.

'This man attacked this young woman,' Logan said, gaze swinging to the marshal. 'There was another one, too, smaller fella, only I wager he wasn't really a fella, was he? Bettin' it was Markello's second, a gal named Mousy.'

The marshal stared at him, the shock on his face telling Logan he had known damn well someone was going after Dawn, but had not expected this outcome.

'Reckon that's only your word,' he said at last, as if scrambling for some explanation. The marshal didn't strike Logan as the smartest pig in the poke.

'Miss Hawthorne will testify to it. She's a witness.'

The marshal cast her a look, one that said he was damned unhappy to see her standing there. 'You provoked him, miss, I reckon. Probably promised him something and wouldn't deliver. See your type a lot. Got me a notion to arrest you both.'

It took only a heartbeat for Logan to lurch across the desk and grab a handful of the marshal's shirt, then haul him half across the body that was lying on the desk.

'You listen here, you lowly sonofabitch. I got damn little tolerance for crooked lawdogs, so you just go ahead and try to arrest either of us. That man in your cell' – Logan ducked his chin at Markello – 'he's not your prisoner by a long shot. You're his. So don't play me for a fool. I aim to kill him for what he's done and if you get in the way I'll kill you, too. As it is now, I can't accuse you of anything more than being an accessory, but I find your hands got blood on them things will change.'

The threat was clear and the marshal nodded a jerky nod. For an instant his gaze flicked to Markello, who stood watching, a smug expression frozen on his lips but a contrary one in his wild eyes. His hand still rested in his pocket, no doubt ready to draw some sort of gun if need be. Logan wasn't entirely sure who the lawdog was more scared of in that instant, but it might have been a draw. That would change the moment Logan left, because Markello would assert his will on the lawman again.

Logan shoved the marshal backward; he landed in his seat and didn't move.

'You find that other attacker and arrest her,' Logan said, backing towards Dawn.

'Go to hell,' said the marshal, now that Logan was a few feet away and some of his bravado had returned. Markello's influence on the man was too powerful to break, but Logan had served notice the ante was upped. 'Get out of here before I decide to arrest you for murder.'

'Doubt you'd live long enough,' Logan said, his gaze going to Markello. The outlaw didn't move.

'Fine lookin' woman you got yourself there, Priest. Hope you plan on sharing.' The outlaw uttered a small laugh and the wildness in his eyes increased.

It was all Logan could do to keep himself under control but Dawn touched his arm, and his composure came back, as if that touch had given him strength.

'Tellin' you once, Markello. You're a dead man.'

'Was the day I was born, Priest. We all are.'

Logan backed towards the door, keeping Dawn behind him in case the outlaw suddenly abandoned his plan and drew. Logan wanted the killer to think about the dead man on the desk for a spell, coddle some anger at the manhunter. Logan needed an advantage and he wagered the outlaw had a very low threshold for being mocked.

The sun had set and a lantern in the marshal's office cast a jaundiced light across the faces of Demarte Markello, the marshal and three others, two hardcases and the woman called Mousy. All sat in hardbacked chairs, except Markello, who stood in his cell, his dark eyes glinting with fury. He hadn't expected Priest to kill his man. Hadn't expected it at all. He had planned on the murder of Priest's woman weakening him, making him easy prey, but something inside the manhunter – some strength of will and power of soul Markello had thought broken

116

– was still alive and strong. And it infuriated him. Made it harder to stick to his gameplan.

But killing Priest outright would ruin everything. When he'd murdered his own folks he had done it too quickly, in enraged bloodlust, and the thrill had been all too fleeting. This time he wanted to savor it. Priest was the only other man, beside his pa, to resist him and he wouldn't have his victory taken from him.

But, confined to his cell, he knew his patience wouldn't last long enough for him to implement his plan unless he released some of the pressure. He was a man given to rage-driven action, one who held to no other scheme than that of gaining control over others. Working this way was hell served cold. Especially after being confined in a cell the past few years. And he wagered somehow Priest knew it too and killing his follower had been an open challenge, mocking defiance.

His fingers curled into a fist and balls of muscles stood out to either side of his jaw. With each day that passed, he reckoned he was closer to losing control completely over the demon screaming within him, though many would have said that happened the day his pa threw him out of the homestead. But this was different. While he might have always been insane by some folks' standards, this time confinement had pushed him close to a line that once passed would destroy his ability to compose a rational thought. He would become a rabid animal, without restraint, and likely be shot down as one. He would lose his power over others, the thing he most craved, along with killing. He couldn't let Priest take that from him. Couldn't let Priest win a second time.

He'd misjudged the sonofabitch. Again. He needed to think clearly, remove Priest's newfound composure. He reckoned he knew who had given him that self-control. Whatever new-found strength Priest possessed, it was fragile and tied to that woman. And that was Demarte's ace.

One he would play after he let off some of the pressure.

Coming from his thoughts, he let out a roar and shook his head violently. Spittle gathered at the corners of his mouth and for a moment he struggled to rein in the demon inside.

After dragging moments, he unclenched his fist and took a shuddery breath.

The others in the room stared at him as he stepped from the cell, their faces expectant, submissive, clearly used to his turns of fury. He surveyed them, the feeling of power he held over them calming him some. They clung to his teat like babies, craved the nourishment of his wisdom and guidance.

'Brothers,' he whispered, pulling his timepiece from his pocket and turning it over in his hand. 'And sister. . . .' He gazed at Mousy, who looked back with laudanum-dulled lust. 'Done been too long since we had us some . . . fun.'

He went to the desk, opened a drawer and drew out his Bowie knife.

'There's a small cabin outsida town,' the marshal said, peering at the outlaw. 'Newcomers, just settlin' in. They don't realize Darkton ain't partial to squatters.'

Markello nodded. 'They'll do. . . .'

He turned to the rest, a grin spreading across his lips and crimson drawing a curtain before his vision.

'They'll do jest fine. . . .'

CHAPTER NINE

Logan Priest heard Dawn Hawthorne sobbing through the hotel room wall and it brought back a flood of memories. Memories of how Serena had cried the day he left.

He sat on the edge of a worn mattress in the tiny room furnished with a small bureau, atop which rested a porcelain wash basin and pitcher, and a rickety table and hardbacked chair. Red-striped wallpapering stained with blood and God knew what else, patches torn off in places, covered three walls, the fourth being bare. The odor of urine and old booze permeated the room, stung his nostrils. But he'd slept in worse, though in a condition in which it had mattered little.

You were trying to protect her.

Hell of a job you did.

How are you going to protect the woman in the next room?

She'd almost been killed earlier today and

Markello was still in that cell, gloating and waiting, likely figuring out a way to make sure the next attempt on her life succeeded.

Logan saw one glimmer of hope. After dumping the body on the marshal's desk and issuing his challenge, he had caught a certain spark of annoyance in the outlaw's eyes. Markello brooked no challenge to his authority, and no resistance to his will. Yet Logan *had* resisted him, thrown down the gauntlet. The killer had not planned for that.

But Logan reckoned any respite gained from his ploy wouldn't last for long. The outlaw would strike back unless Logan found a way to throw him completely off his game. Markello would soon send someone after Dawn Hawthorne and attempt to regain the advantage. And if something happened to her . . . Logan had grave doubts he could maintain the little control he'd achieved over his composure.

You can't let that woman be hurt . . . you have to make her leave.

But would she listen to reason now? He had grave doubts where that was concerned, too.

He stood, went to the door, paused with his hand on the handle. He wondered what she was crying about, guessed it had something to do with her husband, or maybe her earlier brush with death had simply caught up with her.

It occurred to him then that he cared entirely too

much about whatever it was that was saddening her, and he gripped the door handle harder, knuckles going white. Just what was happening to him? Why did he give a damn about this woman he'd known such a short time?

He had a notion the answer was one he didn't want to dwell upon.

Dawn Hawthorne sat on the edge of the bed, sobbing into her palms. The minute she separated from Logan Priest and returned to her dingy room emotion had surged up and overwhelmed her. Those outlaws had nearly killed her. If not for Logan Priest. . . .

She had no business seeking revenge on an outlaw such as Markello. That was a job better left to manhunters like Priest, professionals. She was only getting in the way and risking her life, a life she had not cared a lick about only a few weeks ago. But now she did care and the thought of dying sent a shudder through her body.

You care too much, she told herself. *Taking care of him those two weeks. . . .*

She was falling in love with Logan Priest, and it struck her as somehow unseemly in view of her husband's recent death. She had just been loveless for so long, living a lie . . . were her feelings for Logan just some kind of foolish fancy?

Perhaps. Or perhaps not. It didn't matter. As

much as she wanted to live, to discover whether her feelings were more than morning mist, she still had a duty to her husband, and she would see it through. She had never broken a vow and she wasn't about to start now.

She lifted her head from her hands, shook it, then with a swipe of her arm brushed tears from her cheek. She wished she hadn't left her derringer lying in the alleyway. She considered going back to look for it but that would only leave her vulnerable to attack again. The second attacker – Logan had told her he believed it to be a woman named Mousy – was still out there. Perhaps there were others, as well.

She stood, wrapped her arms about herself, unsure which way to move next. She had to do something. But what? Maybe she *should* go back and look for her gun.

A knock on the door startled her from her thoughts and she drew a deep breath to compose herself.

'Just a minute,' she said in a loud but quivery voice. She sniffled and wiped her face with her sleeve again, before starting for the door.

Logan knocked on the door, having no idea what he was going to say to the young woman to make her ride away from this town and never look back. Funny thing was, the thought of her leaving brought him no pleasure. He wanted her to go, but then again, he did not. That frightened him. He had glimpsed her staring at him, gazing at him the same way Serena used to. With affection.

But affection was impossible for him, no matter the things he felt stirring inside, things he hadn't felt for two years. He had a mission to complete, and beyond that. . . .

He couldn't allow himself to care for her. That was all there was to it.

The door opened and she stood there, her eyes red, tracks of tears still evident on her face.

'Sorry . . . but I heard you crying.' Damn, finding words suddenly felt awkward as hell. 'Everything all right?'

She looked away a moment, frowning. 'I banged my arm on the bureau,' she mumbled.

He ignored her excuse, knowing it was a lie. 'That other one who attacked you . . . I *will* find her and make her pay for trying to kill you, if that's what you're frettin' about. I won't fail again.'

She gazed at him, her eyes softening. 'That's a right different attitude than the one I heard from the man in the saloon earlier.'

He hated the way she read him and at the same time it made him nearly reach out and draw her into his arms.

Before he could answer, she suddenly came to her tiptoes and kissed him. For an instant he let her, tasting her lips on his, lost in the sensation.

Coming to his senses, he pushed her away and shook his head. Embarrassment reddened her cheeks.

'I'm sorry—' she said, voice quivering.

'I can't,' he said, still shaking his head, stepping backward. 'It ain't right. Your husband's only been gone . . . and Serena. . . .'

A tear slipped from her eye. 'It *is* right, Mr Priest. There's something you don't know about my husband . . . there wasn't any love on his part. Our marriage was a lie. But he was a good man just the same and despite his past. And I made a promise to his memory I would see he got peace.' She hesitated, eyelids fluttering. 'And your woman . . . she'd want you to live on, not just give up after you bring down Markello.'

'Damned if you know what you're talkin' about,' he said, tone harsher than he expected it to be, maybe because she was right and he was not ready to admit such to her.

'I do, Mr Priest. I do know. I see it in your eyes. You think you got nothing to live for once Markello pays for what he's done . . . *if* he pays and doesn't kill you first. But you're wrong. You got something if you want it.'

He backed farther away, turned, unable to look her in the eye.

'I'm sorry,' he said. 'I just can't. . . .'

He left her standing there in the doorway, unable to say what he had come to say. He went back to his room and closed the door. Maybe he was still that running coward after all.

CHAPTER TEN

The next morning Logan Priest stepped from the hotel to spot a wagon rattling to a stop in front of the funeral man's cabinet shop down the street. His gaze settled on the back, noting something heaped beneath a canvas. Blood stains, like rust-colored orchids, soaked through the material, and something in his belly plunged.

'Markello,' he muttered, and began walking towards the wagon.

Something had happened during the night, something horrible, and to Logan's mind that could mean only one thing: the outlaw had waltzed out of his cell and along with Mousy and perhaps others had committed some atrocious deed.

In a sudden burst of guilt, he blamed himself, because he had mocked the outlaw yesterday. Logan had counted on that tactic making the killer antsy, perhaps goading him into abandoning his plan and making a mistake. But the dread welling in his belly told him things hadn't worked that way. Markello had taken his anger out somewhere else.

Damnit, he should have anticipated that response. He'd made another mistake and it had cost more innocent people their lives.

A sudden paranoid notion taunted him that it might be Dawn beneath that canvas, but he quickly pushed the thought away. He had heard her moving about her room earlier, before he left the hotel. In fact, he had avoided her by sneaking out, having no desire to confront the young woman after her kiss last night. Because the truth was that kiss had scared him; scared him because he liked it and wanted more, and he had no call thinking or desiring such things with Serena's body still fresh in the ground.

She'd want you to go on. . . .

Dawn's words drifted into his mind and he knew she was right. Serena would want him to love again, abandon his quest for revenge and release the fury he held inside. But how could he?

As he reached the wagon, the marshal stepped off the boardwalk and got in front of him. A sizzle of anger went through his veins and Logan had the urge to grab the man, slam him against a support beam and pound an answer out of his lying hide. A sliver of good judgment prevented that from happening.

'Get out of my way, Marshal,' he said, voice low.

Something in the marshal's dull eyes flickered, acknowledged that blocking him was a damn poor idea. The lawdog moved aside.

Logan went to the back of the wagon, where two men who'd climbed from the driver's seat were preparing to hoist the canvas from the back. He stopped them with a wave of his hand. They glanced at the marshal, who nodded.

Logan pulled a corner flap back, as quickly covering the sight again. Three bodies, those of a man, woman and child, though it was difficult to tell, given the condition. He stepped back, nausea welling in his belly, legs shaky.

'Reckon we've got ourselves an Injun problem,' said the marshal, a smug expression turning his lips. 'I'd wager Comanche, way the heads were cut half off.'

Logan shook his head, having all he could do to hold his stomach down and keep from losing all control over himself. 'This wasn't the work of Indians. There aren't any Comanche in this area, Marshal, and you damn well know it.' Logan's pale-gray eyes narrowed, drilling the lawdog. 'An entire family, Marshal. Wiped out just like that by that monster you got in your cell.'

The marshal shifted feet. 'Markello was in his cell all night, Priest. Saw him there myself. Slept in my chair. Figure these were squatters, so if it t'weren't Injuns that got 'em, then they got some fool angry

129

enough to serve them their fate.'

Logan saw it then, deep in the marshal's eyes. This man was no mere crooked lawdog. He was following Markello without question, condoned the outlaw's murderous rages.

Logan took a step towards him, halting three inches from his face. 'Sooner or later Markello will give up this charade, Marshal. Reckon he figures he's got his plan all laid out, that he can break me like some fool horse fresh off the range. I ain't no horse and Markello can't keep this up. *He* can't do it and you know it as well as I do.'

'You're wrong, Priest.' The marshal said it with very little conviction.

'Am I? He's done the worst he can do to me, short of killing me and I'd almost welcome that. He'll get too full of himself and make a mistake. And when he slips up I'll be there. This time I won't be bringing him in for the law, I'll be burying him. And you right along beside him.'

The marshal's face reddened. 'Suppose I tell him that?'

A thin smile came to Logan's lips. 'Suppose you do. . . .'

A movement on the boardwalk caught Logan's attention and his gaze flicked in that direction. Dawn Hawthorne stood there, her hands over her mouth, face pale, as she stared at the back of the wagon.

Gaze returning to the marshal, Logan brushed past him, jarring his shoulder and knocking him a step sideways. Very little kept him from killing the lawdog where he stood. He knew this man was guilty of abetting, perhaps even participating in heinous crimes and had the young woman not been standing there. . . .

But he preferred that the lawdog took the message back to Markello. A warning that said, make a mistake, you sonofabitch.

He would deal with the marshal later.

'You reckon Markello's responsible for those bodies?' Dawn Hawthorne asked Logan Priest, as they walked along the hotel's foil-papered hallway. A lantern cast a buttery glow across the worn carpet. Outside, dusk was starting to settle. Logan had spent most of the day with the young woman, saying little, but making sure she was not left unguarded. She would be an even bigger target now that Logan had issued his warning to Markello and the marshal.

'No doubt,' Logan said, belly twisting. 'I underestimated him again, I reckon. I wanted to make him antsy, wanted him to make a mistake. Didn't reckon on him killing anyone innocent. He doesn't think or act like a normal outlaw. I got downright lucky the first time I caught him.'

She nodded, went silent, her face washing pale.

The more time he spent with her the more he felt things he struggled to deny. Not only an ever-growing attraction to her, but a weary anxiousness as well. The very thing he wanted to use against Markello, that inability to stick to a plan because the outlaw would grow edgy or overeager with his quarry so close, was grating on his own nerves. Just the thought of that killer sitting there in that jail taunted him, made him want to walk in and put a bullet between his wild eyes.

Like Markello, Logan Priest had never been a chess player when it came to hunting his prey. He'd never applied a maneuvering strategy in his manhunting days, though he'd always been cautious on the trail. He simply tracked down his quarry, then either brought it in or killed it. Most outlaws were a cocky breed, given to overconfidence and bragging, and sooner or later they made a mistake that got them cornered.

Markello was the same, yet different. The outlaw was driven by demons Priest had no desire to contemplate or understand. And when he acted, folks died, horribly. He couldn't allow that to happen again.

'I'm goin' to look around the marshal's place soon as it gets dark enough,' he said as they reached Dawn's room.

She gave him a surprised look, but nodded. 'I'll go with you.'

'No.' Logan shook his head, his tone hard. 'I aim to stop him and the marshal before anyone else gets killed, and that includes you. I best do this alone. I don't come back you ride on out of here and don't look back.' He turned to her, gripped her shoulders and something inside him felt almost alive again.

'I'm . . . sorry,' she said. 'About last night, when I . . . kissed you.'

'Reckon maybe it's the likes of me who should be apologizing. I never wanted to let Serena close to me. I was always scared of that and I gave her excuses about outlaws catching up to me, using her against me, whatever I could think of to keep her at a distance.'

'But you didn't succeed, did you, Mr Priest? I can see how you felt about her. You loved her.'

He nodded, emotion tightening his throat. 'Reckon I did, but it's too late to say it and I'll live with that till my dying day. Just one of the many mistakes I've made over the past few years. Tonight I aim to make up for all of them, least as much as I can under the circumstances. It won't make up for what I did, or didn't do where Serena was concerned, but Markello *will* pay for his crimes. That marshal, too.'

'You talk like a man who doesn't intend to come back. . . .' Her voice had lowered and tears welled in her eyes.

'Go fetch your saddle-bags and head over to the livery. Ready your horse and wait for me just outside of town. I ain't back by eight, you'll know something went wrong.'

She peered at him, suddenly came to her toes and kissed him again. This time he made no move to pull away. He let himself accept the kiss, knowing full well even if he did kill Markello and that law dog, he might ride away and leave her waiting outside of town. He simply didn't know if with this mission finished, one way or the other, that he had enough will to go on living.

A moment later he pulled back and turned, started down the hallway. He could feel her gaze on him, and for a fraction of a moment he wanted to stop and go back to her, forget about vengeance.

But he couldn't. Markello would never let him and this time that sonofabitch was not going to hurt anyone he cared about.

At the far end of the hall a shadow moved and the woman called Mousy peered around the corner. She watched the hotel room door close and a vicious smile slit her lips. She didn't know where the manhunter was off to but Markello wanted the girl, so it didn't matter. This time Demarte wanted her alive, at least for a spell, and Mousy had been waiting for her to return to her room the entire afternoon. The Hawthorne woman was in there alone now, and

Mousy had overheard something about her going to the livery and leaving. That simply wouldn't do. She had seen them kiss too, and that would please Markello. The woman meant more to Priest than they had thought.

A soft laugh trickled from her lips. Her hand went to her pocket and her fingers gripped a cold metal object, drew it out. The object consisted of rings of brass that slipped over her fingers. She would take no chances. She was strong for a gal, but knew how Markello treated those who made mistakes. Those who couldn't follow his orders deserved death, she reckoned, and while she was all too happy to die for the glory of her master, she wasn't prepared to do it tonight.

Dawn Hawthorne closed the door, then went to the window. She watched the darkening street until she saw Logan Priest exit the hotel and head towards the marshal's office. A moment later he vanished into the deepening shadows.

A determined smile filtered onto her lips. He was plumb loco if he thought she was just going to wait for him at the edge of town. She had seen it in his eyes that he didn't plan on coming back, win or lose. But she had also seen a measure of indecision, a chance for them. That would only happen if she didn't let him go, if she fought for something just starting to grow.

No, she was going nowhere, except to help him, and that meant she would need some sort of weapon. Her derringer was gone by now, she reckoned, but she would get somebody at the saloon to sell her their piece.

She went to her saddle-bags, pulled out a roll of greenbacks. Her husband had kept some of the money he'd taken from Markello, quite a sum, in fact. It bothered her that in some ways the money might have been ill-gained, but she had no other way to live for the time being. Helping Logan Priest would put the money to a good cause, however, and atone in a small measure for the acts committed by the outlaw.

She peeled off a number of bills and stuck them in her skirt pocket, then returned the rest to her bags. She reckoned she had little time before Logan made some kind of move, so if she planned to back him up it had to be in minutes rather than hours.

Just as she started towards the door, a soft knock came.

She paused, a bolt of anxiousness going through her. She doubted Logan would have come back so soon, but no one else knew which room she was in – unless someone had followed them. . . .

'Who is it?' she asked, voice tentative, face paling.

'Management, ma'am,' a voice came back. The voice was husky, low, and through the door she couldn't tell whether it belonged to a man or a young boy.

Kill her. . . .

The words spoken by the second attacker in the alley suddenly jumped into her mind, the one who had escaped. That voice . . . it was the same.

'What do you want?' she started to back up, her mind scrambling for options. She was on the second floor, so she couldn't go out the window, and there were no other exits in the room.

'Man named Priest sent me up to tell you there's been a change of plans. You ain't to meet him outside of town.'

Her eyes narrowed and her heart stepped up a beat. How could Markello's second possibly know that?

The door burst open. Damnit, she had not bothered to lock it when she came in, intending to go right back out as soon as she saw Logan disappear.

'Going somewhere, missy?' the smallish woman asked, a smug expression on her face.

She didn't look all that big, just kind of small and dirty, like some street waif, so maybe she could—

Dawn lunged towards the bureau. She grabbed the porcelain water pitcher and tried to swing it around.

Mousy charged her, got her arm up to deflect the blow. The outlaw girl's free hand swung up and something hard crashed into Dawn's chin. Blackness

137

flooded her mind and her legs buckled. She was vaguely conscious of an echoing laugh as the floor rushed up to meet her, then nothing more.

CHAPTER ELEVEN

Logan Priest merged with the shadows after he crossed the street, and headed towards the marshal's office. Few folks were out and about, and no one paid him much attention. He reckoned after the murders of the previous night most would be behind locked doors come dark. The few he did notice appeared to be cowboys on their way to the saloon, some already half in their cups.

Logan had his doubts Dawn Hawthorne would follow his order to await him at the edge of town. She had acquiesced all too easily and from his time with her he judged that was not her personality. No, she would likely do something foolish, such as follow him.

That meant he had to act fast and take out Markello and the marshal tonight.

Logan slipped into the alley beside the marshal's office, gaze sweeping behind him, making sure no one was following. Senses alert, he made his way down the alley, darkness swallowing him. The darkness was too thick for his gaze to penetrate more than a few feet, but he made out the bulky shapes of old crates stacked along the building's walls.

It occurred to him Markello might not leave anything to chance since Logan had put him on notice, and would not rely on just the marshal to protect him while in that cell. Other men, or Mousy, might be posted outside the office. Logan didn't spot anyone, but that manhunter's sixth sense was sending prickles through the hairs on the back of his neck.

You don't have to do this. . . .

Serena's voice entered his mind and he hesitated. Yes, I do, he thought. I do have to do this. I have to give you peace and I have to give myself peace.

What about the guilt? How did he live with that? Did he live at all after his mission was complete?

A few days ago he was prepared to end his own life after he ended Markello's. Now. . . .

Could he leave Dawn Hawthorne the way he had left Serena?

Things had been so much less complicated when he was drinking his life away, hadn't they?

No excuses this time, Logan, he told himself. That young woman is offering you a reason to go on, and Serena would want you to.

You leave her to her own after this it's because you are too

140

much of a coward to face your own feelings.

He shook off his distraction, knowing it was the wrong time to be dwelling on such thoughts.

He paused, the shiver going through the nape of his neck again. He glanced behind him, then forward, but still saw nothing. Yet. . . .

On the trail, two years ago, he would have trusted his senses more. A manhunter, like a cougar, knew when someone was stalking him. Right now . . . right now he wasn't sure of anything, except that the outlaw had to pay for his crimes.

He edged up to a window, from which subdued lantern light penetrated into the alley no more than a few feet.

His hand went to the handle of his Peacemaker as he peered into the office. Anger surged through his veins at the sight of two men, but he forced himself to control it. Markello and the marshal stood in the center of the room, the outlaw out of his cell. That was enough for Logan. He started to draw his gun. He would take no chances with that madman, not this time.

He moved away from the window, heading for a back door he had spotted the last time he'd been in the office.

A sound came from behind him, the scuffing of a boot and he suddenly knew his manhunter's sixth sense had been right: Markello had posted other men.

Logan spun, his hand jerking his Peacemaker from its holster. He had an idea where the sound had come from and swung in that direction.

A man, bathed in shadow, stood there, having come from behind the pile of old crates, a gun raised. Logan triggered a shot. The blast came before the man, startled by his discovery, could fire. The other hadn't intended firing, Logan reckoned, probably just getting the jump on him, but that didn't matter. Far as he was concerned anyone in league with the outlaw belonged in a pine box.

A bullet punched into the man's chest, sending him careening backwards into the crates. The attacker hit the ground on his back, gun flying from his grip. The blast sounded like thunder, the tumbling crates only a little less noisy.

Logan cursed. Those inside now had warning and that removed any advantage he might have had.

He whirled, ignoring the man lying on the ground. The man's raspy breath told Logan he was breathing his last and no longer a threat.

Logan lunged towards the back door, but something crashed into the side of his head. He stumbled, pitched forward. Face first, he slammed into the dark ground, his Peacemaker flying from his grip. A second later, a boot thudded into his face, ending his consciousness.

*

The next thing Logan became aware of was being sprawled on the floor in the marshal's office. Markello, the lawdog and one other man stood over him.

'Fetch Mousy,' Markello said, peering at the man standing to the left of the marshal, the one Logan figured must have bushwhacked him in the alley. 'Tell her to bring that girl here.'

'Here?' Surprise jumped onto the marshal's face. 'What the hell are you thinkin'? I thought you were just gonna kill her and leave her in Priest's room.'

'Change of plans since Mr Priest kindly delivered himself to us.' Markello gazed down at Logan, who couldn't make his limbs function yet. The side of his head throbbed and thunder raged in his brain. 'You done pegged me right, Priest, if it's any consolation. I was going plumb crazy waiting out my plan. I wouldn't have made it much longer.'

Markello knelt before Logan, hand slipping into a pocket and bringing out a small gun. 'But I knew you'd cave before I would. I saw it the moment you looked at that gal yesterday. Doubt you even realize it yet yourself what you feel for her, but I knew it would send you after me before I could get to her again. Reckon I won't enjoy your suffering as long now but I'll take pleasure in it just the same. Least I will once we get that gal here.'

Markello stood, handed his gun to the marshal. 'Cover him,' he said, ducking his chin to Logan. He reached into a pocket and brought out his watch, began turning it over in his hand, then glanced at his follower. 'Go.'

The man nodded and went out.

CHAPTER TWELVE

'I've done waited a long time for this moment, Priest,' Markello said, fingers worrying the watch in his hand, their movement more agitated now. The wildness in his eyes became rabid, glittering with madness.

Logan, some of the feeling coming back into his limbs, tried to push himself up but Markello's boot snapped out, crashed into Logan's jaw and sent him over onto his back. Ringing pain splintered through his teeth. His head pounded. But he didn't give a damn. He was more worried about Dawn Hawthorne and what Markello would do to her once his man brought her here.

I won't lose another. . . .

A surge of adrenaline coursed through his veins and determination cleared his mind. He gazed up at Markello, whose face held a curiously detached look, despite the wildness in his eyes. The man was utterly mad, Logan thought. Plumb loco. Worse

than he recollected from their first meeting years
back.

The outlaw's fingers played over the surface of
the gold watch, rubbing it with an almost frantic
motion now.

'Go to hell, Markello,' Logan said, then spat a
stream of blood as he rolled onto his side.

Markello uttered a thin sound that wasn't quite a
laugh; it might have been something made by an
animal on the verge of attacking its prey.

The marshal, who with a shaking hand held
Markello's gun on Logan, shifted feet, eyes darting,
face pale. He clearly wanted to put a bullet in Logan
and end any chance of something going wrong. But
Markello wanted to play with his prey, taunt it.

The outlaw went to the window, peered out into
the street, nodded, as if seeing something that
pleased him. He turned back to Logan. 'Hell ain't
such a bad place once you been there a while, Priest.
I done learned to live there after my folks sent me
off, but livin' in Hell's what makes a man strong,
learns him his wits.'

'You're not strong, Markello,' Logan said,
propping himself up onto an elbow. 'You're a sorely
diseased sonofabitch.'

A half-smile formed on Markello's lips. 'I'm
inclined not to disagree, but appears to me your
convictions have weakened you where mine just
made me stronger. Those years ago. . . .' Markello

hesitated, face reddening slightly and rage brewing behind his eyes. 'Those years ago, I wondered what made Logan Priest so strong he's able to resist me when others, others like our friend the marshal here, jest succumbed to my influence practically the moment I laid eyes on them. I done got the power of the Devil, Priest. I'm blessed with such. And the marshal here, he's done got a weak soul.'

The marshal glanced at Markello, as if he were about to protest, but the outlaw gave him a corrosive look that stopped him instantly.

'But you ain't strong, Priest,' Markello continued, slowly walking to the desk. 'Least not no more. Maybe not since you met your woman. See, lovin' something . . . lovin' something don't make a man strong. I learned that when my folks set me out. Lovin' something corrupts a man, makes him weak, gives others all the advantage they need to break a fella's will. That's what happened to you, Priest. You got soft on someone and discovered a coward in your soul. I reckon in your mind you might have even told yourself by leaving that gal you were doin' right by her. But you weren't. You were just givin' in to your own weakness.'

Logan's belly cinched and emotion tightened his throat. Markello was trying to get to him and doing a fine job of it. Logan swore some dark force emanated from the man, as if the Devil did indeed possess him.

But that wasn't true, was it? Markello relied on others' demons to give him power. He read men, somehow, read them, pinpointed their Achilles' heel, then used it against them. He preyed on outcasts like Mousy or those corrupt like the marshal, and figured himself right powerful. But he was no more powerful than a politician or minister spouting false words aimed at exploiting human failings and fears. That's what he was aiming to do now, reach into Logan's mind and manipulate his guilt, use the blame Logan had placed upon himself. But Logan refused to let that happen.

Logan's eyes met the outlaw's. 'You're wrong, Markello. If you had an ounce of anything human left inside you you'd know it. You're nothing more than a dead man inside and I reckon a damned sick and lonely one. The Devil has no true companions, does he?'

Markello's eyes got wilder and Logan knew the outlaw was on the edge. He was used to manipulating men and when it didn't work his mind refused to accept the fact. If Logan could push him. . . .

Markello uttered a laugh that sounded utterly disconnected from reality. His dark eyes narrowed and for a moment he appeared somewhere else, far away. Then his face tightened and his gaze focused on the marshal.

'Put him in the cell and lock the door.' Markello

went behind the desk, opened a drawer and drew out his Bowie knife. The blade was caked with blood, likely from last night's killings. The killer tucked his watch into a pocket, then caressed the blade, drawing a finger along it as if savoring the gritty sensation of the dried blood.

The marshal took a step towards Logan, motioning with his gun for him to get to his feet.

'I'm gonna carve up that gal in front of you, Priest, 'fore I kill you. I'm gonna do it slowly, too, piece by piece while she screams. Way your first woman screamed when I sliced her throat—'

With the outlaw's words every bit of willpower Logan had to keep his control vanished. Maybe Markello was right, and he had become weak in some ways, because just the thought of what that monster had done to Serena and what he would do to Dawn was enough to shatter his composure.

He lurched to his feet, faster than the marshal expected, and the lawman, tense, jerked the trigger of his Smith & Wesson. The blast thundered in the room, nearly shattering Logan's eardrums. A bullet plowed into his shoulder and spun him, but with it came a piece of luck, for it whirled him towards the outlaw.

An instant later the door flew open and Mousy, Dawn and the man Markello had sent to fetch them entered the office.

Mousy and the other man, both of whom had a

grip on Dawn's arms, tried to go for their guns. Dawn suddenly jerked her arms free and made a grab for Mousy's gun, which was halfway out of its holster.

The marshal, startled by his own shot and the door opening, jerked from his spell and twisted towards the door, his gun swinging to aim on Dawn.

Dawn had grabbed Mousy's gun and yanked, bringing it free of the holster. She jammed a finger through the trigger guard and fired. A blood rose blossomed on the lawdog's chest. The gun dropped from his limp fingers and he crumpled to his knees, a spray of crimson coughing from his lips. A second later he toppled face first to the floor.

Logan checked his lunge towards the outlaw as Mousy tried to regain control of her gun. The other follower drew his weapon, started to aim at Dawn.

Logan swooped, scooped up the dead lawdog's piece and came up as if it were one move. He triggered a shot. A black hole appeared in the follower's sternum, right above the heart. The man flew backward, slammed into the wall, rebounded, then crashed to the floor.

Logan had no time to try for Mousy, and the woman was too close to Dawn to risk firing. He swung, knowing Markello hadn't remained idle; the outlaw had whipped around the desk, was bringing up his knife.

Logan tried to swing the gun but couldn't get it

around in time and an invading weakness from the blood pumping from his shoulder wound began to swarm through his body.

Markello's knife flashed downward and Logan barely got out of the way. The blade tip split the fabric of his shirt, drawing a thin slash of blood across his chest.

Markello's eyes had gone completely wild, frantic, as if whatever sanity he had was nothing more than a façade. Now that he had lost control over the situation, he was no more than a cornered animal.

Markello slashed the knife backhand and Logan ducked. The blade swept over his head, but the outlaw instantly brought up a knee, slamming Logan in the chin and knocking him bolt upright. The gun tumbled from Logan's fingers. Head whirling and agony flashing through his jaw, he tried to grab for the weapon, but Markello kicked it out of the way.

'Not . . . that . . . easy. . . .' Markello said, his voice gravelly, tinged with rage.

The outlaw jerked the knife up, then down, toward Logan's chest.

Logan sidestepped, taking another slash in the opposite shoulder, but getting his arm up enough to deflect a fatal wound.

Logan let out a yell and threw himself at the outlaw, sending Markello back against the desk. The outlaw tried to slash downward again with the knife, but Logan managed to get a grip on the man's wrist, twist it sideways.

Christ, the sonofabitch was strong, Logan thought, as the man forced him backward and managed to straighten. Or perhaps Logan had merely gotten weaker over the past two years. It made no difference, because if he didn't get that knife away from the killer Dawn would die with him.

He jerked up a knee, burying it in the outlaw's crotch. He had kept hold of Markello's wrist, and twisted it more as he forced the man backward again, onto the desk. He slammed the outlaw's wrist against the edge of the desk, but Markello clung to the knife with almost inhuman strength.

Spittle bubbled from the corners of the outlaw's lips as he tried to force Logan back up. Logan banged the outlaw's wrist against the edge of the desk again, harder, then a third time.

Markello's fingers opened and the knife fell from his grasp.

Logan made a slight mistake, then. With the knife no longer a threat, he let up on the outlaw a fraction and Markello took full advantage. He surged upward, flung Logan off him.

Logan hit the floor, rolled, more surprised than stunned. He quickly leapt back up to his feet, but the room swayed, and his vision blurred an instant.

Markello was already lunging for this knife.

Logan, out of pure survival instinct, dove for the

outlaw, slammed a shoulder into him. Markello stumbled sideways, hit a wall, but seemed to possess an almost superhuman ability to recover. He whirled, threw a punch as Logan came in. Logan tried to duck, but it caught him a glancing blow, making his legs wobble.

Near the door, Dawn was struggling with Mousy and had managed to keep the gun from Mousy's grip but couldn't hold onto it. It landed on the floor and the spike-haired outlaw grabbed at Dawn.

Dawn snatched one of the girl's wrists, but Mousy jabbed a punch with her free hand that banged across the top of Dawn's head. Dawn's legs nearly buckled. Mousy surged atop her, still hammering with her free fist, forcing Dawn to her knees.

Logan caught it in a glance as his head cleared and he instinctively came up with a vicious uppercut. The blow collided with Markello's chin with a sound of a gunshot. For an instant the outlaw's wild eyes dulled.

Logan threw a short straight punch, slamming it home into the outlaw's teeth. Markello staggered, but nearly as quickly recovered and buried a fist in Logan's belly.

Logan managed to buckle to avoid the full impact of the blow, but nausea swelled his gut and bile surged into his throat. If he vomited he was done. He would not be able to breathe and against Markello that would be fatal.

Save her. . . .

The thought of Dawn dying sent a rush of adrenaline through his veins and he let out a roar. He came up with another uppercut. The blow raked Markello's face, throwing him off balance. Logan followed up with a left hook that thudded against Markello's temple. The outlaw's eyes clouded.

Something in Logan snapped. In a blood-red haze the past careened through his mind and he relived every horrible moment of opening that box and seeing Serena's severed head. His ice-gray eyes glinted with a chilled resolve, frozen insanity, and he swung and swung and swung.

Each blow crashed into Markello's face, mashing his nose with a spray of blood, shattering a cheekbone with a brittle eggshell sound and mangling his lips to a pulp. Markello's eyes glazed and he wavered, though he still refused to go down.

Breath searing out in heavy gasps, every muscle shaking, Logan didn't let up. He couldn't. Dawn's life depended on it; justice depended on it.

He kept pounding the killer, battering him, until Markello at last fell.

'You sonofabitch!' he yelled, slamming a boot into Markello's face once the man was on his knees. 'You killed her! You killed Serena!'

He kept kicking and almost nothing could have stopped him from pummeling the outlaw to death in that moment.

Except a short plea that somehow penetrated his rage. His eyes cleared as his head swung back to Dawn. Mousy was poised atop her. The outlaw girl had somehow recovered her gun and was jamming it against the young woman's forehead.

'No!' Logan yelled, diving suddenly, grabbing Markello's Bowie knife and coming up with it.

Mousy hesitated, glanced back, saw him with the knife and tried to swing her gun around.

Logan hurled the blade. It thudded into Mousy's chest. The boyish follower arched, the gun dropping from her fingers. Dawn shoved and Mousy pitched sideways, landed on the floor and lay still.

Logan's breath came in searing gasps. Sweat streamed from his forehead and beneath his arms, down his chest. Weakness flooded his limbs, blood loss from the wound in his shoulder taking its toll.

Dawn got to her feet, came over to him. She placed a hand on his shoulder. 'It's over,' she whispered.

'No!' he snapped, pushed her away. Shock played on her face as he spun back to Markello. The outlaw was stirring.

'Never again, goddamnit,' Logan said. 'Never again.' He went to the gun Mousy had dropped, picked it up, then returned to Markello.

The outlaw looked up at him, dark condemnation in his eyes. 'Do it, Priest,' he said, words low, gurgling, but mocking. 'Do it. Make yourself into me. . . .'

155

Logan aimed the gun at Markello. His hand shook, knuckles going white as his grip tightened. Dawn stepped back, her eyes wide.

'I ain't like you, Markello. I never will be. But I won't let you walk out of a cell and kill another innocent human being again.'

Markello started laughing, an insane cackle of a sound. 'Kill me in cold blood, Priest? You ain't that strong. . . .'

No, Logan – Serena's voice sounded in his mind – *that won't give me peace. . . .*

His hand shook harder on the gun; his finger twitched on the trigger.

'I wanted to see him die as much as you, Mr Priest,' Dawn's voice came softly from beside him. 'He will this time, if you bring him in and I know now that's the right thing to do.'

Logan looked back to her, saw her pleading face. 'What he done—'

'I know.' Dawn frowned and a tear slipped from her eye. 'He'll pay for it, though I reckon we both know it will never make up for the pain he caused. But I don't think your woman would want this. I don't think my husband would, either. He tried to make things right; he changed. Maybe I don't owe him vengeance, just justice.'

Logan looked back to Markello, the outlaw's bloody grinning lips mocking him and he damn near pulled the trigger.

'Not strength, Markello,' he said at last. 'You don't need strength to kill a man. You need weakness and it would be weakness killing you this way. I ain't . . . I ain't a manhunter anymore. I'm just a man who lost something he cherished; you took it from me. But I won't let you take whatever human part of me I still got left.'

Logan lowered the gun.

Markello started to laugh, insanity completely taking over.

Logan kicked him in the teeth. He reckoned his resolve wasn't perfect.

Two weeks later, Logan Priest, his arm in a sling, his shoulder wound healing, stared at the body swinging from the gallows. He hadn't needed to return the outlaw to his old cell. The town council, led by the barkeep who'd been temporarily appointed the new marshal, had met and decided the outlaw's fate. Logan and Dawn had both testified.

Demarte Markello had hanged half an hour before but Logan hadn't been able to take his eyes off the swaying corpse. In some deluded corner of his mind he wanted to make sure the killer was truly gone, that he didn't have some supernatural ability to return from the dead. Foolish, he knew, but the man had had an almost inhuman ability over others – who was to say he couldn't sway the Devil?

He'd also spent time contemplating what lay ahead. His manhunting days were over, but possibly the man he had once been might return. He would forever suffer with guilt over Serena's death, and for the death of other innocents at Markello's hands, but perhaps he'd come to realize it wasn't entirely his fault. He had brought the man to justice. Justice had not done its part.

Still, he couldn't help but blame himself, at least for leaving Serena, exposing her to the danger of his way of life. She would have told him that choice was hers, and maybe she was right. But had he stayed. . . .

'You don't know that.' A voice came from behind him and he turned to see Dawn Hawthorne standing there.

'How the hell d'you know what I was thinking?'

'Was obvious from the look on your face, Mr Priest,' she said softly. 'But I would have known anyway. I asked myself if I could have done something to save my husband, instead of staying in that cellar. Maybe I could have. Or maybe it wouldn't have made any difference. He'd still be dead and likely I'd be dead too.'

He frowned, looked back to Markello's body. Dark feelings crawled up inside him but with them came warm new ones. He no longer saw a future that held nothing.

He felt her hand touch his shoulder. 'You can't

change what's been, Mr Priest,' she said. 'Just what's to be.'

He nodded. 'Reckon you're right. But it won't stop me from grieving over it for a hell of a long time.'

'You still planning on riding off without me, Mr Priest?' she asked, her voice shaky. Maybe there was one thing about him she couldn't read and that almost pleased him.

He turned to her. 'Can't say I didn't rightly consider it.'

'But you won't.' She smiled a thin smile.

Damn, she had read him again. So much for little victories.

'I won't.' He took her hand, started leading her back towards the hotel.

'You reckon I can stop calling you Mr Priest now?' she asked, her smile widening.

He let out a small laugh. 'I reckon I've grown kind of fond of that, leastwise if there's a Mrs Priest to go with it.'

She peered at him, raised an eyebrow. 'That a proposal, Mr Priest?'

'It's a future, Miss Hawthorne. . . .'